Multi-Orga

By Lucy Felthouse

Table of Contents

The Sound of Silence

"Yvette!" Jack snapped. "Are you even listening to what I'm saying?"

"Yes, Sir!" I'd only missed a bit. Maybe a couple of words. And it wasn't my fault.

"So what's the problem? Are you uncomfortable? Would you like a cushion?"

"No, Sir. I'm fine, thank you. It's just..." As another noise filtered in through the double glazing, I was unable to stop my gaze slipping in that direction.

"What—?" Jack strode past me, all stompy and masterful.

I allowed myself a shiver of pleasure at his demeanour. He was sexy when he was grumpy, though naturally I didn't enjoy it when he was grumpy with *me*.

He peered out the window to see what had distracted me. "Neighbour is mowing his lawn, that's all. Can't very well go around there and complain about that, can I?" he muttered.

Jack stepped back in front of me. "The window is closed, Yvette. I can't really do any more than that." He shrugged.

"It's okay, Sir. He'll be done soon. I can ignore it. It's not that loud." Ever since he'd given me that *look* and ordered me into the bedroom, my pussy had ached, and I had yearned for his orders, to do his bidding. To please him. I certainly didn't want to *dis*please him by allowing the next-door-bloody-neighbour's garden maintenance to get in the way of our scene, but it'd be tough to remain entirely focused with that racket going on.

"Hmm. All right, then. Let's continue. So, where were we?"

I hoped like hell that was a rhetorical question, because I'd been distracted enough by the noise outside that I hadn't, in fact, heard all of what he'd said. I bowed my head and waited, mentally keeping my fingers crossed that Jack would answer his own question. Luckily for me, he did.

"Come here, take out my cock, and suck it."

"Yes, Sir!" I almost got carpet burns on my knees as I eagerly shuffled forward. I reached out and undid his zip. After slipping my right hand through the gap, I manoeuvred until my fingers closed around his shaft—which was rigid, red hot, and irresistible.

Carefully, I popped his cock out through the opening in his boxers and trousers, where it stood proudly, looking just as irresistible as it felt. All purple and swollen; raring to go. Licking my lips, I pumped my fist up and down his length a couple of times, before closing my mouth around his glans. Immediately, the delicious musky, salty taste of him hit my taste buds and I hummed happily and prepared to start sinking further onto him.

Just then, a high-pitched roaring sound reached my ears.

Jack picked up on my flinch. Stepping back—and slipping his dick out of my mouth in the process—he exclaimed, "Oh, for heaven's sake! It's really distracting you, isn't it?"

I sat back on my heels and pouted. "I'm sorry, Sir! I can't not hear. If I could switch my ears off, trust me, I would."

Jack's expression softened. "Hey, it's okay. It's not your fault. It's just... kinda ruining what we've got going on here."

I bit my lip. "Yeah, I know. But what are we supposed to do

about it?"

Jack opened his mouth to reply, then closed it again. I could almost see the light bulb appear above his head. Quickly, he tucked himself away, then turned and headed for the door, throwing over his shoulder, "Back in a minute."

I frowned, wondering what the hell he was up to.

Fortunately, I didn't have to wonder for long. Jack soon returned, grinning broadly. "I've got the solution to our problem, my love."

"Y-you have?" He didn't seem to have anything with him— but wait, maybe he did. His right hand was closed, as though holding something.

"Yep. *Voila!*" He lowered his hand to my eye level, then opened it. Sitting on his palm were two tiny metal things, with black rubbery-looking ends.

"Wha—are they ear plugs?"

"In a manner of speaking, yes. But they're so much better than the regular kind. Put these in and you won't hear a thing."

Tentatively, I scooped them off his hand. "But that means I won't be able to hear you speak. I won't know what you want me to do."

Jack's grin widened. "I'm sure I can make myself understood. Shall we give it a go?"

"Yeah... all right."

He explained how to fit the plugs, then waited while I did so.

One ear done; already the world's volume had been turned down. When I popped in the second, it was indeed as though my ears had been switched off. It was bizarre—I could hear myself breathing and swallowing, but otherwise... nothing.

Jack waved, drawing my attention. He put up his thumbs and arranged his face into a question.

I nodded.

He gave a curt nod back, and smiled. Then he gestured towards his crotch, raised an eyebrow. He'd been right—he could make himself understood.

I soon had my husband's shaft in my mouth once more. This time, though, there were no distractions. I poured my entire being into sucking and stroking Jack's luscious dick. He was my only focus—nothing else mattered. Nothing else *existed*. The downside was I couldn't hear any sounds he made, any moans, groans, expletives.

But that made me all the more aware of his other reactions; the tensing of his thighs, the jerk of his hips, the hands he'd fisted in my hair. Each subtle twitch, the increase of precum seeping onto my tongue, told me he grew ever closer to climax. And I was ready.

Suddenly, as I bobbed up and down on his saliva-slick shaft, Jack froze. His hands tightened in my hair, sending sparks of pain dancing across my scalp. Then his cock twitched between my lips, and juices flooded my mouth. I swallowed them down happily, eagerly, buzzing with delight and arousal at his climax, secretly hoping I might soon be allowed one of my own.

I carried on swallowing and gently sucking until Jack's climax abated, then let his cock slip from my mouth. Looking up at him, I pointed to my ears, raising my eyebrows in query.

He nodded.

Carefully I removed the plugs, immediately missing the quiet.

Jack asked, "How was it for you?"

"Totally amazing! I missed not being able to hear you, but I was so aware of everything else, how you moved, how you felt—"

"Good. But you can't keep them. I need them for work." He held out his hand.

I narrowed my eyes. "Well, then, you'd better order me some, hadn't you?"

"Consider it done. And just think what it'll be like if I spank, whip, or flog you while you're wearing them." He gave me a wicked grin. "You won't be able to hear what's coming, or when."

The thought made my heart race, and my mouth went dry. Clumsily, I pushed the plugs into Jack's outstretched hand. "Go. Now," I said, not even caring that I wasn't supposed to be the one giving orders. "And for God's sake, pay the extra for express delivery."

One Plus One

Jayne Simmons took a deep breath, fighting to slow her racing heart. She dug her fingernails into her sweaty palms.

Deep down, she knew perfectly well nothing bad would happen—it was just her own personality and anxieties making her want to turn and run.

Why couldn't the conference have been at a hotel that offered room service? Being all but forced to attend was bad enough, but she'd consoled herself with the fact that at least outside the hours of the talks and lectures—where she'd keep herself to herself—she could retreat to the sanctuary of her room.

But that wasn't an option. Not unless she wanted to starve to death. Which she then idly considered as a possibility.

She let out a heavy sigh and urged herself to step over the threshold before she started attracting attention by dithering in the doorway. One of the main reasons she'd even *become* an accountant was because it was a job that would, by and large, allow her to work around her paralysing social anxiety. Meeting new people had always been a problem for her, right from childhood. But being holed up in an office with nothing but a computer for company? Heaven. Give her spreadsheets over humans any day.

If she could just slip in, eat, and slip away again unnoticed, she'd be delighted. She'd have to interact with the restaurant staff, but she could just about deal with that—would have to, unless she'd changed her mind about starving to death.

Being unnoticed was an art she'd perfected over the years. Her given name, with its superfluous 'y' in the middle, had helped earn her the unoriginal nickname "Plain Jayne" since junior school and, rather than rebelling against it, she'd embraced it. If she was plain, uninteresting, then nobody would notice her. For the most part, it worked, and to say she enjoyed a quiet life was one hell of an understatement.

That clearly wasn't going to be the case tonight, however. For no sooner had she entered the crowded dining room, than she was noticed.

"Jayne?" said a deep, male voice. "Jayne Simmons, is that you?"

Fuck! Her heart rate ramped up again as she looked around in a panic to see who had spoken. Who the hell could possibly know her here?

Her hurried search came to an end when a man she presumed was the owner of the voice emerged from the line of people waiting at the service counter and approached her. She frowned and observed him through narrowed eyes.

As he grew closer, her stomach churned and her pulse thudded even harder—much more of this and she'd have a bloody heart attack. Suddenly her brain acknowledged what her body—or her cardiovascular system, at least—had already surmised. She knew *him,* too.

What was more, she'd had a crush on him for three whole years at university.

Clive bloody Woodward.

"Hi," she squeaked. She had gone all lightheaded, and had a strong suspicion the smile she thought she was aiming in Clive's direction was actually a grimace. Poor bloke would soon regret speaking to her.

Clive smiled. "Jayne—do you remember me? Clive Woodward? From university. I'm sure I've changed a lot!" He chuckled and ran a hand through his greying hair. "You haven't, you jammy so-and-so. Other than your hair being shorter, you look just the same."

"Of course I remember you," she replied breathlessly, wishing desperately for the ground to swallow her up. She was inching closer to a full-on panic attack, and having her old crush being all chatty and charming wasn't helping. *Come on, Jayne, get a fucking grip, woman! You know him, remember? This doesn't count as meeting a new person, even though you haven't seen him for twenty years.*

The thought calmed her ever so slightly, and she managed to add, "It's lovely to see you. You look great. Life's obviously been treating you well." She clamped her lips shut then, impressed with herself for making conversation.

"Thank you. You look fantastic, too. Though, if you don't mind me saying, a little flushed. Are you feeling all right?"

Jayne nodded frantically, although the inferred 'yes' was the exact opposite of what she actually felt. She sucked in a breath and waved a hand at the room. "It's just… all this." She hung her head, growing more embarrassed by the second. "It's a bit… much."

Immediately, Clive's expression grew serious. "Shit. I'd forgotten. I'm such an idiot. I'm going to gently take your arm, Jayne, all right?"

She nodded and croaked, "All right."

"Come on," he said warmly. "You're going to be just fine. I've got you."

Clive led her over to an empty table tucked away in the furthest corner from the buffet counter, where it was quieter. He pulled out a chair and helped her to sit. "Just keep breathing, Jayne, okay?" He took the seat beside her and poured her a glass of water from the carafe on the table before handing it to her. "Here you go."

Jayne took the glass with what she hoped was a grateful smile, rather than another grimace. Clive was being so kind, so patient with her—he certainly didn't deserve to have her pulling faces at him.

Especially since, after all these years, he'd actually remembered her little—ugh, who was she kidding, it was huge!—issue and was being very considerate about it.

Jayne took several careful sips of the water and, by some miracle, the panic began receding. Clive remained silent, exuding patience. When their eyes met, he flashed an encouraging smile.

Her heart flipped over as she realised Clive was, in fact, having a calming effect on her. His very presence made her feel like everything was going to be all right. As an added bonus, he *didn't* make her feel like a nuisance, or a freak, or like she was overreacting. He was just kind, caring, and understanding of her needs. That hadn't happened in... well, forever. She'd always been made to feel her issues were something she should just be able to "get over".

Didn't they realise, if it were that simple, she would have

done it by now? Did they think she *wanted* to be like this? Wanted to freak out every time she stepped or was pushed outside of her comfort zone? Yes, she loved her job, and had managed to build a life for herself where any situations which might trigger her anxieties were kept to a minimum. But she *did* want to be like everyone else— to have friends, relationships, a partner.

Sex.

God, did she want to have sex! She had a year on *The 40-Year-Old Virgin,* and ridiculous didn't even begin to cover it. What kind of person didn't even manage to ditch their virginity at university?

A person, she reminded herself, whose social anxiety was so bad that she didn't go to parties, didn't get drunk, didn't lose her inhibitions. And clearly the less seedy way of just meeting a nice guy, dating him, then eventually sleeping with him was never going to happen. On the upside, she'd graduated with first-class honours— inevitable when the hottest affair she'd had was with her textbooks.

She'd long since resigned herself to living without sex—with another person, anyway. So why now, after all these years, was she thinking about it? Why now, when the man she'd lusted over for three interminable years sat in front of her, still gorgeous, still charming, still perfect? He'd been out of her league then, and he was certainly out of her league now. That and he couldn't possibly be single.

A surreptitious glance at his left hand told her he either wasn't married, was divorced, or didn't wear a ring. So she was none the wiser.

Story of my fucking life, or what? Not like I was going to make a move on him, anyway.

She put the glass down on the table, then, a totally alien bravery filling her, met Clive's eyes again, forcing herself to maintain contact, not to look away. "Thank you, Clive. I really appreciate your help. I'm feeling much better now."

His smile widened, the gesture making his blue eyes crinkle at the corners. Jayne's heart thumped again. "You're welcome. Are you ready to get something to eat now?"

She shifted her gaze to the counter, then back to him, and shook her head. "No, I don't think so. I've lost my appetite."

"I can come with you. I haven't had anything yet. Or I could go and get something for you, if you give me an idea of what you like, or don't like."

Jayne's cheeks heated and she shook her head again, then looked down at her hands. "Honestly, it's fine. I'm really not hungry. Thank you, though. I think I'm just going to go back to my room. I'll get something at breakfast time."

Clive frowned. "And what if you have another panic attack then? You can't spend the whole conference not eating. You'll be ill."

Shrugging, she replied, "I'll have to cross that bridge when I come to it." She stood. "Anyway, thank you again. I guess I'll see you around?"

He got to his feet. "Can I walk you back to your room? I'd like to make sure you get there all right. You still look peaky."

"O-okay. Thanks." If it had been anyone else, she'd have

been eager to get rid of them and be alone. But Clive was different. He didn't inspire the same fear other people did. He never had, actually, but it was only now that she was realising it.

She scurried for the lift. As she stuck her finger on the call button, she sensed Clive stepping up beside her.

"Jayne?"

"Yes?"

"Am I making this worse for you?"

Sweat prickled on her palms. "W-what do you mean?"

"I'm just keeping an eye out for you, but you ran out of there like a bat out of hell. If you don't want me to walk you back to your room, it's all right. I understand. I know you prefer your own company. I'm just concerned about you, that's all."

"Actually," she blurted, "you're not making it worse. You're making it better. I'm not sure how, or why, but your presence gives me the sense that everything is going to be all right. That sounds so cheesy—I'm sorry." Her cheeks burned.

The lift pinged its arrival, and the doors slid open. Clive held out a hand, indicating she should go in ahead of him. As she did, he chuckled. "You have nothing to apologise for, Jayne."

"I don't?" She selected her floor on the control panel and then stepped back as the doors closed and the car began to move.

Clive shook his head. "Of course not. I'm flattered."

"Okay," Jayne replied, not knowing what else to say. Silence reigned, then, as the lift transported them up to Jayne's floor. It continued as they exited the lift and made their way along the corridor and up to the door of her room.

She retrieved her key card from her bag. "Right," she said, meeting Clive's eyes with some difficulty, "I'm all set. Thank you for walking me back."

With a small smile, he replied, "That's quite all right. It was my pleasure. You're sure you're going to be all right now?"

She nodded. "Positive. I'll see you tomorrow."

"I hope so." Then he turned and walked back towards the lift.

For some reason, Jayne didn't immediately unlock the door and rush into her room. She was frozen in place, watching him walk away. Then, suddenly, despite knowing she would indeed see him the following day, she called out, "Clive, wait."

He spun around and returned to her, concern etched into his features. "What is it? Are you all right?"

"Fine!" she chirped. "I'm fine. I just wondered... do you want to come in for a nightcap?"

Clive narrowed his eyes and tilted his head. Jayne's heart sunk. She'd been so brave, and he was going to say no! She took a step back, butting up against the doorframe and fumbled to get her key card into the slot. "F-forget it. Forget I said anything. It was stupid. Please, just..." She trailed off as the card slipped from her grasp and tumbled to the carpet. "Shit!"

"Stop," he said firmly. "Just stop. Let me get that."

She cringed against the wall as he retrieved the key card, then effortlessly used it to unlock her door. He held it open for her. "There. Now, about that nightcap. If the offer is still on the table, I'd be delighted to accept."

"Y-you would?" Her eyes widened, and relief flooded her

body.

"Yes. Why do you sound so surprised?"

"I don't know. I just... I'm not good at this kind of thing."

"What kind of thing is *this,* exactly? I want to make sure we're on the same page here, so there are no misunderstandings."

She opened her mouth to respond, but just then the other lift arrived and disgorged a group of people who turned and made their way in Jayne and Clive's direction. "Can we... discuss this inside? In private?"

"Of course. After you." He continued holding the door as she entered the room, then followed her in and closed the door behind them.

She hurried over to the sideboard, then swore as a thought occurred to her. She'd only brought one glass with her! Letting out a heavy sigh, she turned and gasped when she saw how close Clive was. "S-sorry, I just realised I've only got one glass. Obviously," she added in a tone thick with sarcasm, "why the hell would *I* need two? Plain Jayne, super freak."

"Hey," Clive snapped, taking a step towards her. "Stop that right now. You are not plain, nor are you a freak. Let me go and get one of the glasses from the bathroom. You open the wine. All right?"

She nodded sheepishly and, this time as she watched him walk away, her reasons for calling him back and inviting him in for a nightcap became clear. Whether he was available or not, simply spending time in his company wasn't wrong. And, for her, since spending time in *anyone's* company was such a rarity, even *wanting* to, that when she'd discovered how safe and secure Clive made her feel, it would have been even stupider if she *hadn't* called him back. He was a sweet, caring man, and chatting with him was vastly preferable to spending the rest of the evening alone—something she'd *never* been able to say before.

It was a no-brainer.

With that revelation, she turned and set about opening the wine and pouring a glass. By the time she'd done that, Clive had reappeared with the other glass—albeit a plastic tumbler, rather than the proper wine glass she'd brought with her—and brandished it with a smirk. "I'm ready for my nightcap."

Jayne filled Clive's glass, and they walked over and sat on the end of her bed. "So," she began, leaping in before her newfound courage deserted her, "that private conversation we were going to have... about the *thing.* I mean..." She stopped, blew out a frustrated breath, then took a sip of wine. *You've got this far. Go on!* "Clive, are you single?"

His response was a surprised splutter. He held his free hand over his mouth for a moment before responding, "Sorry, you took me by surprise there. I like this direct side of you. Yes, I'm single. Are you?"

Her instinct was to give a sarcastic response, but he didn't deserve her self-aimed ire, so she simply replied, "Yes. So... are we on the same page?"

Raising his eyebrows, he took a sip of his own wine and swallowed. Then, "Depends what page you're on. My page is that I like you. I find you extremely attractive and, providing you're okay with it, I'd very much like to kiss you. I've wanted to do it since our university days, but had no idea how to broach the subject without freaking you out."

"Then," she said quietly, "I guess we're most definitely on the same page." Taken over by that brave part of her she hadn't known existed until recently, she carefully removed Clive's glass from his hand and took it, along with hers, and placed them on the sideboard. Then she returned to her perch on the end of the bed. In the back of her mind she was shocked she wasn't panicking about Clive's proximity, but the rest of her brain was more concerned with getting closer still.

As though he read her mind, Clive scooted over so the sides of their thighs were touching. His eyes full of intensity, he asked, "Are you sure about this, Jayne? We've technically known each other a very long time, but we also don't know each other very well. I don't—"

She pressed her fingertips to his lips to shush him. "I want this. And I'm fucking delighted about wanting it. I feel normal for the first time in forever. I want to embrace that feeling, run with it, not pick it apart and wonder about it."

He gently removed her hand from his mouth. His lips were quirked in a half-smile. "Fair enough. But can I just ask one question?"

"Yes."

His eyes glinted with mischief. "As well as feeling normal... do you feel horny?"

The bark of laughter escaped before she'd had chance to think about it. "Yes, I do. What are you going to do about it?"

"This." Suddenly serious, he cupped her cheek, then leaned down and captured her lips in a kiss.

Jayne was overwhelmed with sensations. The sensual warmth of his lips against hers, his hand on her face, his tongue peeking out to explore her mouth. Add to that the scent of his cologne and the hormones whizzing around her body, and she was in danger of meltdown. She'd given up hope of ever losing her virginity, much less to a man she really liked.

Hoping Clive wouldn't be able to tell she had no idea what she was doing, she slipped her arms around his neck and kissed him back.

He responded with a growl from deep in his throat, which ramped up the dull ache between her legs. When he cupped her breast, she let out a sound of her own, something between a growl and a purr. It spurred Clive on, and he began to gently squeeze and caress her breast as their kiss grew more frantic. Their tongues entwined and danced together, and before long Jayne was so overcome with need that when Clive pushed her back on the mattress, she didn't bat an eyelid—figuratively or literally.

They continued kissing and touching each other, breaking apart every now and again to remove an item of clothing. When there was only underwear left, Jayne paused. "Clive? Do you... I mean, I don't—"

"Relax. You know earlier, when I said 'I've got you'? It counts here, too. I have protection, don't worry. So just you lie back and—"

"Think of England?"

"You'd better bloody not!" he said indignantly, eyes flashing. "In fact, when I'm finished with you, you won't be able to think at all."

Her tummy fluttered. "I like the sound of that."

Smiling now, Clive ditched his boxer shorts, then retrieved a condom from his wallet. After getting back on the bed, he pressed the package into Jayne's hand and moved in for a kiss, murmuring, "See? I've got you."

Scorching heat blazed where their skin contacted. She moaned against his lips, then gently pushed him away, her chest heaving as she fought to breathe. "Can we... now... please?"

"There's no rush, is there?" His brow furrowed.

"Yes... this time," she murmured, the scorching heat now blazing on her cheeks.

Realisation dawned on Clive's face, followed by hesitation, and finally, a gentle happiness. "Your wish is my command. But—"

"Yes, Clive, I'm bloody sure!" she exclaimed, smiling. Why wouldn't she be sure? It was a cliché, but in this case, literally nobody had ever made her feel this way before—physically, emotionally, mentally. She was about to do something that should have been terrifying, and yet all she felt was eagerness, delight.

Need.

"Can I... see you properly, Jayne?" He nodded down at her body, still in knickers and bra.

Wordlessly, she removed the bra and knickers and threw them on the floor.

Clive looked her up and down, his eyes darkening with lust.

"Fucking hell, you're so beautiful. I'm the luckiest man alive."

Her grin reached from ear to ear. "And I'm the luckiest woman. Now make love to me, please."

His response was to position himself between her legs. With one hand he fisted his rigid cock, and with the other he stroked her pussy. Finding her wet and ready, he raised his eyebrows. "Just when I thought you couldn't possibly get any sexier. Gimme that condom, gorgeous."

She complied. He made short but careful work of putting it on. Juices seeped from her pussy as she watched him. God, this was really happening! With Clive bloody Woodward!

Jayne smiled up at him as he climbed on top of her, bracing his weight on his arms before reaching down and positioning himself against her entrance. He pressed a brief but heartfelt kiss to her lips. "I'll take it slow. If you want me to stop, please, *please* say so. I've got you."

Want him to stop? Was he mad? She was on the cusp of losing her virginity to a man she adored. Even if it was a one-night stand, it would still be the best thing that had ever happened to her. But somehow, she suspected it wouldn't be.

She nodded, and he moved. Maddeningly slowly, he pushed inside, her wetness easing his passage. She gasped and wrapped her arms and legs around him, holding him tight as tiny bolts of lightning zigzagged through her. *Oh my God, there's nothing normal about this. It's fucking incredible!*

As she'd expected—she was a virgin, not a moron—there was a miniscule pinch of discomfort, and then he was in, sliding in, and Christ, he felt good. Amazing. She groaned and gripped his firm buttocks, pulling him harder into her.

If he was surprised, he didn't show it. He just gave her what she wanted—more. After a couple of long, slow thrusts, he steadily picked up the pace until they were frenziedly rutting, like animals, their cries spilling into the room.

Her pleasure built and built, spiralling ever higher until she teetered on the very edge of climax. "Clive, I'm going to come soon... are you?"

Without faltering in his thrusts, he nodded. "I've been holding on!"

"Well... ahh... you only need to hold on... a second... longer!" Her breath was stolen from her as her orgasm hit. She bucked and swore and moaned, the sensation of her internal walls gripping Clive's thick cock the most amazing thing she'd ever experienced.

Somewhere in the dizzying heights of bliss, she was aware of Clive coming with a shout. Together they were overwhelmed by pleasure, and together, they came back down to earth. But there was no bump, especially not when Clive's first post-climax words, slightly slurred, were, "So does this mean you're willing to date me, Jayne? Because one taste of you, mind-blowing as it was, is nowhere near enough."

"You're joking, right?" she quipped. "Now I've got you, I have no intention of letting you go. I can't promise I'll be easy to be with, mind."

"That's all right, sweetheart. I've got you."

She smiled and kissed his sweat-damp forehead. "I know."

Behind the Scenes

Carmen did her best to keep skin-to-skin contact with Lucas to a minimum. It was difficult, but for the most part she managed to make sure it was only the tools of her trade that touched him; makeup sponge, brush, eyebrow comb, and so on. Thank fuck male actors didn't (usually) go in for eyeshadow and mascara. She'd *have* to touch him then—hold his chiselled chin as she swept colour over his eyelids…

She gulped. He was right fucking next to her. If she lost concentration, brushed her skin against his for more than a millisecond, she was done for. She'd spontaneously combust, she just knew it.

She'd considered asking the head makeup artist if she could work with someone else—perhaps claim he made her uncomfortable, or something. But nobody would believe that. Every straight woman on the planet lusted after Lucas Forbes and would kill—literally, in some nuttier cases—to be in her shoes. He was charm personified. Besides, she'd be crazy to give up her position— having her name attached to such a huge star's was the only way to progress in her career.

I'd like to attach something to him, all right, she thought, pausing for a second to catch her breath as she put down the foundation and sponge, and picked up the face powder and brush. Not that he needed it really, any of it, he was flawless to start with.

Lucas automatically closed his eyes when he saw what she was about to do, and she had to stifle a contented sigh. She'd damn well miss him if she transferred, too. Not only was he the sexiest man on the planet—according to several magazines as well as her—he was a joy to work with. He was kind, polite, courteous… not at all what many people would expect of a Hollywood star. And yet he was a dream. A perfect dream.

No, she decided, *I'm not giving him up. He's not mine to give up, of course, but I'm not handing this job over to someone else. I'll just have to suck it up and stop lusting over the man. Get him out of my damn head.*

It was impossible, and she knew it, but she *had* to keep a lid on it. For the sake of her career.

"Are you all right, Carmen?" His southern American accent always made her weak at the knees—just another one of his charms. God damn him for talking—didn't he know he was making things worse? "You're awful quiet today."

She smiled sweetly—despite the fact he still had his eyes closed—doing her best to battle the blush that threatened to flush her cheeks, and failing miserably. Although he couldn't see her reddened face, she didn't want to risk it. It was practically a neon sign screaming how she felt about him. "I'm fine and dandy, thanks Lucas. Just a little tired, that's all."

"Well, you need to take better care of yourself then, sweetheart. I don't know what I would do without you."

His words were sweet, lovely, perfect—there was that word again—and Carmen sucked in a hasty breath before replying, trying her best to remain calm. "Thank you, you're very kind."

"I mean it," he said, his eyes popping open and meeting hers, full of intensity. "You're the best makeup artist I've ever had. I'm real glad you work for me."

They weren't touching, but now she *was* in real danger of spontaneously combusting. He wasn't being sexual, not in the least, and yet at that moment, she wanted him more than ever before.

"Well," she blustered, using every iota of willpower to pull herself together. "You flatter a girl. But I'm fine. Let's get you ready for this camera."

Lucas gave a single nod, then closed his eyes again. Nice as it had been, Carmen was glad the conversation was over. Giving in to her attraction would be a great way to lose her job! It was essential she remained professional and only let her fantasies run wild in the privacy of her own bedroom.

She finished making Lucas up, and wished him luck—as she always did—as he left the room and headed out into the studio proper. Through the crack in the door she saw him immediately surrounded by people from the costume department, lighting department, sound department… Everyone wanted a piece of Lucas Forbes.

Slumping into the chair Lucas had vacated, Carmen continued to watch what was going on. Lucas handled the team with his usual kindness and professionalism. She couldn't hear what was being said, but could tell from gestures and body language that he was permitting everyone to do their jobs, and thanking them for it.

It was no wonder he was considered to be the world's sexiest male. And the vast majority of the voters had never even met him. If they did, it would be Beatlemania all over again, with women fainting left, right and centre. And she was the lucky woman who got to be up close and personal with him on a regular basis.

Carmen grinned, realising she should be happy with her lot. There were people in much worse jobs, people *without* jobs, and some doing what she did but with horrendous employers—divas and arrogant pigs. She was the one who got to *touch* Lucas Forbes, talk to him, laugh with him…

God, how she wanted to get him naked and touch him all over, fall into bed with him and press her naked breasts up against his chest… and other things.

She lost awareness of all but her fantasy, retreated inside her head. Closed her eyes. Allowed a naked Lucas to invade her mind, to caress her naked body, to want her.

In the real world she spread her legs and slipped a hand beneath her skirt. Already an intense heat emanated from her crotch, and her naughty thoughts had barely even gotten going yet.

She used one hand to pull the gusset of her panties to the side, and the other to touch herself. To slowly, gently stroke her rapidly-swelling pussy lips, to gather juice from between them and slick it over her aching bud. She'd gone from zero to horny in seconds, and it was all Lucas's fault.

She let go of her panties, leaving her other hand playing with herself, and reached out to the table next to her, patted it until she found what she was looking for. Well, groping for.

Her thickest makeup brush was usually for applying face powder, taking the shine off a client's skin. But now she had a much better use for it. A much more *erotic* use. She gripped the brush near its bristles and guided the other end between her legs. Pushing it past her thickened lower lips and inside her, she sighed happily, enjoying the sensation of being full.

"Need a hand with that, sweetheart?"

The oh-so-familiar voice crashed through her fantasy like a bulldozer through a sheet of paper. Her eyes flew open and she shrieked, cursed, then died of embarrassment right then and there. Or at least she *wished* she'd die of embarrassment, wished the ground would swallow her up... anything that would mean she wasn't sitting, spread-legged with a makeup brush inside her pussy and Lucas Forbes right in front of her.

She wanted to tell herself that at least he couldn't read her thoughts, didn't know she'd been fantasising about him, masturbating over him. But it didn't lessen the shame at being caught in such a compromising position. Her face was so hot it had to be almost purple.

"I... I... I..." It was the best she could do. Realising she'd frozen in place, in that lewd position, she yanked the brush from her cunt and snapped her legs shut.

Lucas smirked, then turned and closed the door behind him, before twisting the lock. "What's the matter, Carmen?"

She couldn't answer. Literally. Fear and humiliation had paralysed her tongue, stopped her brain from providing anything useful. Stopped her thinking, full stop.

Then Lucas did something totally unexpected. He walked over to where she sat and knelt down in front of her. Without a word, he removed the brush from her hand and put it on the table. Then he placed his hands on her knees, pushed her legs open, and let out a hum of approval. "Somebody's wet. I can smell you from here. And now I want to eat you. Any objections?"

He looked up, an expectant expression on his face. She met his gaze, but couldn't do anything else. He raised an eyebrow. After several more long seconds of silence, she managed to choke out a reply. "N—no. No objections." She shook her head rapidly, emphasising her words.

"Well then, that's great." He slowly moved his hands up her legs, inching closer to her crotch.

Carmen didn't realise she'd tensed up until her muscles began to scream with the effort. She made herself relax, or as much as one could with Lucas Forbes's hands and head growing ever closer to one's sex. She watched as he hooked his fingers around the gusset of her panties, just as she had done, and pulled them out of his way. Immediately, he shoved his face up against her pussy, slid his tongue between her labia, and moaned as he tasted her.

Even though the sound he'd made had clearly been one of pleasure, of approval, she couldn't prevent her blush. Lucas Forbes was licking her pussy, for heaven's sake! How was a girl supposed to be cool about that? She was cool *with* it, of course—fucking delighted, in fact—but she couldn't act like it was normal, like it was just a day in the life of being Carmen Montero.

Ugh—she was thinking way too much. She should just enjoy what was happening, while it was happening. Pulling in a breath through her nostrils, she tried to chill out. To concentrate on Lucas, on what he was doing. After a few seconds, she actually achieved it. Only then did it hit her how skilled he was at going down on a woman. Her nerve endings were on fire, her abdomen was tight and her hormones raged. God, any second now and she was going to come all over his face.

She couldn't stop—once her climax was imminent, it was nigh on impossible to prevent its arrival. And if she was honest with herself, she didn't want to. She let the pleasure overtake her. Lucas played deftly with her cunt, his tongue and lips licking and sucking at her clit, his fingers pumping in and out of her, just as the makeup brush had done. She edged closer and closer to the precipice, her entire body tingling, and felt as though she were floating. On a cloud, perhaps. Cloud nine.

Then, with another suck and thrust from Lucas, she was undone. She stuffed her fingers into her mouth to muffle her screams and tumbled into bliss. She was aware of Lucas slipping his fingers from her, and her internal walls rippled around nothing as she bucked and twisted in the chair, juices gushing onto the cushion and Lucas's waiting tongue.

After a couple of minutes, she came down from her natural high and grinned goofily at Lucas. His expression mirrored hers, and the sheen of wetness around his mouth made hers drop open with shock. Had that *really* just happened? Had one of the hottest male actors on the planet today *really* just made her come all over his face? While they were at work, no less!

She cleared her throat. "W-what are you doing here? I mean, why did you come back? Aren't you meant to be shooting?"

"There was a technical fault, and the team aren't expecting it to be fixed for another hour or so. I figured I'd come here and chill out. Instead, I found you… fucking yourself with a makeup brush. I couldn't resist taking over. I hope you don't mind."

Blinking stupidly, she shook her head. "Why the hell would I mind? But I have to ask… why did you do it?"

Lucas frowned. "What do you mean, why? Why not? You're a beautiful, sensual, sexual woman, and I've wanted you for a long time. I was trying to stay professional, but seeing you like that… well, let's just say you broke my resolve, big time."

"Oh. Oh!" She didn't know what else to say. Was he teasing her? Or just flattering her? What the hell did a man like him want with a woman like her?

"Carmen," he said, pulling her from her thoughts. "Would you mind awfully if we finished what we started?" He stood up and cupped his crotch, the bulge there immediately apparent.

Oh, to hell with it. He could be fooling around, just after sex, and she was convenient. But right then, she didn't care. How often did a girl get the chance to have sex with a smokin' hot superstar?

As he kissed her, she decided it was nowhere near often enough. And as he murmured sweet nothings into her ear, she hoped that would change.

Suddenly, the future looked bright. Orgasmic.

In Search of Bookcases

Whenever I'd thought about sugar daddies in the past, I'd always envisioned gross, wrinkly old guys, dripping with tasteless jewellery and wearing clothes far too young for them.

All that changed when I met Declan. He mooched into the furniture department of the upmarket West London department store I was working in and altered my perception forever.

He was impeccably dressed in a designer suit and as he drew closer to me, I felt my eyebrows raise of their own accord. He really was sex on a stick. He was clearly loaded—hello, he was in *this* department store, wearing *that* suit—but he was no diva. He had no entourage, no harassed-looking assistant. It was just him, shopping.

Or at least I guessed he'd be shopping. Men don't often wander knowingly into my furniture department if they're not looking to part with some cash—and lots of it.

He glanced in my direction, then headed straight towards me. As he approached, I flashed him my widest smile. And yes, before you ask, I *was* on commission.

"Hi!" I said, trying not to melt as his new proximity revealed sexy eyes full of mischief and a smile to die for. He had perfect teeth, and dimples which threatened to have me swooning onto the nearest disgustingly-high-priced sofa. He also smelled good enough to eat.

"Hello," he replied, appraising me with that cool, blue stare, "I'm Declan, and I hate shopping. Can you help me buy some furniture and be on my way as quickly as possible?" The lilt of his Northern England accent took me by surprise. In my line of work it was easy to get bored of the snooty Queen's English types. This guy had only uttered a few syllables and already I hung onto every one.

"Sure," I said, a little disappointed that we'd only just met and already he couldn't wait to get away. I tried not to take it personally. After all, he'd just admitted he hated shopping. It wasn't his fault I could have listened to him talk all day. "I'm Sophia, by the way."

I held out my hand. Obviously a well-brought-up gentleman—despite his down-to-earth demeanour—Declan took my hand, twisted it and pressed a kiss just above my knuckles. I battled with a blush, and failed miserably.

"I'm delighted to meet you, Sophia." Then, releasing my hand and encompassing the department with a sweep of his arm, "Shall we?"

I might have worked in a department store, but I'd been well brought up, too.

"After you," I said, then fell into step behind him as he looked around, taking full advantage of the opportunity to check him out. And, it has to be said, his rear view was just as attractive as the front one. Sadly, his suit jacket covered his arse, but there was still plenty to admire. I wore heels, yet he was still a good few inches taller than me, with a full head of cropped light-brown hair. Despite the fact he had probably twenty-five years on me, none of it was grey. I found myself hoping it wasn't dyed. That wouldn't mesh with the hot-and-rich-but-still-normal persona I'd invented for him.

Just as I was enjoying a fantasy about sinking my fingers into said hair and holding on for dear life as he ate my pussy, he stopped abruptly. I halted too, putting a hand against his back to stop myself careening into him.

He spun round, but not before I'd gotten the impression of solid muscle beneath that suit. I snatched my hand away, my face colouring once more. "I'm-I'm sorry," I blustered. "You should really put your brake lights on when stopping so suddenly!"

I immediately wanted to kick myself for coming out with such utter rubbish, but Declan's face lit up and he let out a guffaw.

"You're right," he said, pressing his hand to his chest in acquiescence. "I'm sorry, Sophia. I should have given some indication I was going to make an emergency stop. But, well, it was an emergency."

He pointed to the section of the store which we were now standing alongside. "I want that," he said, quite seriously. "Can you sort that out for me, Sophia?"

"Um, well," I replied, flustered again under his gaze, "I don't mean to be picky, sir, but which items would you like?"

Set up as it was, the 'sitting room' had everything; wallpaper, curtains, tables, a sofa and matching chairs, bookcases... you get the picture.

"Everything." He paused, looking at the display. "Actually, not everything. The curtains are hideous. And we're going to have to find more suitable bookcases than those—they're nowhere near big enough."

"Okay," I said, desperately trying to pull myself together. I wasn't some inexperienced, idiotic shop assistant, after all. I just wasn't used to customers being so direct. And sexy.

"Right," I said, flipping open the pad I'd just retrieved from my shirt pocket. "Let me just get my pen."

Typically, I couldn't find it. I patted my pockets, checked my hair—I've absentmindedly poked my pen into my hair more times than I can remember—and sighed. "I'm very sorry about this, sir. Let me just—"

"No need." He produced a beautiful Mont Blanc from his inside pocket. "Use this."

"Nice," I said, before I could stop myself, "I've got one quite similar myself."

I pulled a face that clearly indicated I was lying, and Declan laughed again, his dimples and twinkling eyes doing funny things to me. It was no wonder I was turning into a gibbering wreck. I mentally shook myself and moved to the display, noting down code numbers and totting up prices in my head as I went. I bit my lip. I'd be able to buy myself a Mont Blanc from the commission I'd rack up at this rate.

"Okay," I said, heading back to where he stood, watching me intently. His hands were in his pockets, causing his trousers to pull taut over his crotch, displaying a sizeable bulge. And it wasn't his wallet. I tore my gaze away and beamed at him.

"Right," I said brightly, ignoring the growing ache between my legs, "let's find you a bookcase and some curtains. Or would you prefer blinds?"

Declan shrugged. "I'm not bothered if I don't have anything. Nobody's going to be looking through my window. Except perhaps the window cleaner."

"Just a bookcase or two, then. Let's see, shall we?"

I walked away then, letting Declan follow me. I nodded curtly to other colleagues and their customers as we crossed paths, but all I was really aware of was the man behind me.

"So," I said, slowing my pace and turning my head to address him, "how big are we talking, exactly?"

Which put my foot squarely in my mouth. Cue more mental self-flagellation. "The bookcases, I mean. How big do you want your bookcases?"

I stopped walking and turned to him, barely restraining myself from putting my head in my hands. Honestly. It was a good job my boss hadn't been around to hear the exchange. I'd have been dragged into his office quicker than you can say 'disciplinary.'

Mercifully, Declan didn't laugh this time. I didn't think I could take any more embarrassment. Much more blushing and my head would explode.

"Well," he said, his dimples a dead giveaway of his mirth, "I do have an awful lot of books. I'm not even sure how many. So I'd need very big ones. Very big *bookcases*, I mean."

Bastard! He was teasing me, and, if I wasn't mistaken, flirting with me. He had to have realised by now that I fancied him.

I tipped him a grin and started walking again, looking for the biggest bookcase I could find. Soon, I found one.

"Ah-hah," I exclaimed, heading into the fake office and indicating a gorgeous pine structure. "What do you think to this one?"

Declan approached, nodding approvingly. He ran his hands

over the wood in an almost sensual manner—which sent my mind right back into the gutter—and turned to me. "I like it. Do you think it'll go well with everything else I'm ordering?"

I looked at the bookcase. It was beautiful, as bookcases go. It was sturdy and well-made, yet attractive and plain enough to fit in with any decor. I made my play. "I think it'll fit perfectly. Do you think it's big enough?"

Declan quirked an eyebrow, obviously unsure whether I'd meant to throw out that double entendre or not. Bringing his fingers to his mouth, he tapped his lips and frowned slightly, as if deep in thought. Before I had time to wonder what he was playing at, he spoke. "I'll take three."

My eyebrows almost disappeared into my hairline. My next pay packet was going to be very healthy indeed. "Great! I think they're going to look gorgeous. Even better when they're all full of books."

He grinned at me then, his eyes crinkling at the corners. It made him look older, but somehow even more attractive. "You love books too, huh?" he said, and although it was a rhetorical question, I answered him anyway.

"I sure do. If I had the money, I'd buy three of these and fill them up, too."

I realised my gaffe too late. The words had already left my mouth. Bollocks! I knew the rules and etiquette; you should never talk money like that with people, especially if they've got lots of it. I held my hands out placatingly. "I'm sorry, sir. I really am. I didn't mean to be so rude. I just meant—"

"Shut up, Sophia," he said gently, halting my verbal diarrhoea. "I'm not one of your stuck-up customers. I'm just a bloke with a few quid. I know what you meant. Now let's get this stuff ordered and arrange for my delivery, shall we?"

Relieved he wasn't mad, I nodded and double-checked the code on the bookcase before indicating Declan should follow me to the computer desk. We sat, and I input everything in silence, painfully aware he was watching me. I was also painfully aware that my cunt was still throbbing and in desperate need of some relief. I managed not to fluff anything up, and then I asked for his delivery details.

I wasn't surprised when he gave me an exclusive-sounding West London address. I even kept calm when the computer delivered the final total, and I told him the figure.

He whipped out his wallet without so much as batting an eyelid. *Fuck, just how loaded is this guy?* Even the celebrities seemed to be surprised at how much they were spending sometimes.

The snap of a Diamond Card landing carelessly on the desk answered that question. Gripping tightly to my sense of professionalism, I picked up the card, pushed it into the machine and did the necessary before handing it to Declan. He input his pin number swiftly, then handed the terminal back.

A few torturous seconds passed when I wondered if this was some cruel joke and that the card would be rejected, forcing Declan to admit he was in fact, completely broke.

Suddenly, the machine whirred into life and churned out Declan's receipt, which I slipped into one of our fancy receipt wallets and handed to him with a smile. It slowly died as I realised this was it. He'd paid, everything was sorted, and now he was going to leave.

We stood, and Declan said, "Well, Sophia, thank you for making that as painless as possible. I'll think of you when I'm arranging my books on my lovely new shelves."

I raised my gaze to his, unsure whether he was flirting, or merely being polite. I smiled, and he took my hand and planted another gentlemanly kiss on it, leaving heat scorching across my skin in its wake.

"Perhaps," he dropped my hand once more and reached into his jacket pocket, "you'll come and see the room when it's all done?" He pressed a swish business card into my hand. "I'll cook you dinner, as a thank you."

I gaped at him, unsure what to say. Cook? Dinner? For me?

Clearly desperate to avoid an awkward silence or a rejection, Declan cleared his throat and said, "Well, think about it. My personal mobile's on there. You can reach me any time."

He was gone before I had chance to respond.

I was sure I hadn't imagined the emphasis on *any time*. *Was* he flirting with me? If he'd been a guy my own age, I'd say he was, but what did such a hot older guy want with someone like me? I'm just a normal girl.

Then I got it. Maybe that was the point. I remembered that despite his bank balance and status, Declan was a normal guy. A very well-mannered guy, but normal nonetheless. Maybe he just liked me and wanted to see me again? He'd seemed pretty keen to show me his book collection. Hopefully he wanted to show me a lot more besides. I grinned at my own wanton thoughts.

When I pulled myself back into the present, I realised I was still holding his business card. And that wasn't all. Clutched in my other hand was his Mont Blanc pen. My mouth went dry, and my heart pounded.

I considered rushing after him—he couldn't have gone far—but I stopped myself. The more I thought about it, the more I believed he'd left the pen behind on purpose. I'd been brandishing it around enough, there's no way he'd have forgotten that I had it.

I decided I'd take it to him later, after my shift had finished. Returning his property was the decent thing to do.

***

When I arrived outside Declan's building, I couldn't help but let out a low whistle. He may not have classified himself as posh, but his residence certainly was. There was a great deal of wealth in this building. I wondered if they'd even entertain the idea of letting a commoner like me in.

I walked in, confident that I looked the part, at least. I'd gone home directly from work and gotten showered and changed. I was wearing an expensive outfit—staff got first dibs on clearance items in the store—so I knew the steward at the desk would at least talk to me.

"Hi." I beamed at him. "I'm here to see Declan Merrells, please."

"Certainly, ma'am," he replied, picking up a telephone situated on the desk, "and who may I say is calling, please?"

"It's Sophia."

After a brief exchange, the steward nodded at me. "Mr Merrells will be down presently."

"Thank you."

I stood awkwardly, waiting. There were four lifts in the lavish lobby, so I had no idea where he would appear from. I fiddled with my handbag, which contained the infamous pen, and fidgeted nervously.

He turned up just in time to avoid me doing a runner. I heard a 'ping' from one of the lifts and the doors swished open. Declan walked out, looking like he couldn't be more pleased to see me. I also noted that he didn't appear at all surprised, either.

"Sophia." He walked up and planted a kiss on my cheek. "How lovely to see you!"

Declan turned to the steward and nodded. "Thank you, Adam. Come, Sophia."

Then he headed back towards the lift as if it were the most natural thing in the world. He pressed the button, then held out an arm when the doors slid open once more. "After you."

Normal guy or not, Declan had beautiful manners. I stepped into the lift, feeling a little weird as the doors slid shut. My heart fluttered as I wondered if I was doing the right thing. I mean, I hardly knew the guy, and yet I'd turned up at his apartment block unannounced. And now I was going upstairs with him.

When he turned to me with a smile, my fears melted. Not to

mention my pussy. He too, had changed, and now wore casual attire. Jeans and a T-shirt, to be precise. He looked much more relaxed in this outfit, or perhaps it was because we were on his terrain. Regardless of reasoning, he looked divine. He'd recently showered as his hair looked a little damp, and in the enclosed space I got a whiff of shampoo. My pussy gave a leap as my mind wondered just what he'd look like naked under a spray of water.

"Now," he said, startling me from my almost-fantasy, "you must excuse the mess. I've only just moved in, as I guess you realised from my shopping spree. I can assure you, I don't usually live like a pig."

I was given an excuse not to answer him as the lift intoned its arrival at our destination floor. The top floor, I realised. No wonder he wasn't worried about anyone seeing through his windows. He lived in the sodding penthouse! He ushered me out of the lift and rather than us ending up in the corridor I'd expected, we were *in* his apartment. I hadn't noticed what he'd done in the lift, but he must have a special key or a code or something to make the lift go to this floor.

Moving into the space, I gaped. If he thought *this* was living like a pig, then what the hell would he make of my place? Granted, there were boxes and things lying around, clearly waiting to be unpacked, but still... it was stunning.

Declan interrupted my property lust by clearing his throat. I turned to see he held a bottle of wine and two glasses, which he wiggled at me. "Wine?"

"Oh!" I said, his sexiness making me flustered again. "I'm

sorry, I'm not here for a social visit. I just came to return your pen."
I pulled my bag off my shoulder and began rooting around in its
depths for the Mont Blanc.

"Nonsense," he replied smoothly, "you came all this way to
return my pen, the least I can do is give you a glass of wine. You're
not driving, are you?"

I wasn't. I didn't even have a car—there's not much point in
London. I shook my head, still looking for the damn pen. Finally, I
pulled it out of the bag with a cry of triumph, but not before
snagging my emergency knickers and flipping them out onto the
floor. I gazed, horrified, at the tiny pile of lace lying so brazenly on
Declan's wooden floor.

Cheeks flaming, I snatched the thong up and stuffed it back
into my bag, then waved the pen at Declan, who stood there looking
incredibly amused. Part of me wanted to slap the grin off his face,
but a much bigger part wanted to kiss it off.

He held out an empty glass to me. I took it, and allowed him
to pour me some wine, then took a healthy gulp. I needed something
to steady my nerves and curb my humiliation, after all. I swallowed
just in time, though, because Declan's next comment would have
surely had me spitting wine all over the place.

"So," he said, still smirking, "was that underwear for my
benefit, or do you always keep knickers in your bag?"

I simply stared at him.

"Come on, Sophia. Help me out here. I went to all this
trouble to get you here, the least you can do is let me know if I'm
barking up the wrong tree or not. I *thought* you liked me, but my

radar could be off."

"No," I said, more forcefully than I'd intended. He looked crushed, obviously getting the wrong end of the stick. "I mean, no, you're not barking up the wrong tree. I like you, too. A lot."

"Well, I'm glad we got that cleared up. They were very nice knickers, by the way. I'm sure they don't leave much to the imagination, though."

"Wouldn't you like to know?" I retorted, embarrassment making me defensive.

"Now that you come to mention it, I'd love to. May I?"

I said nothing, just nodded. Declan put his burdens down on a randomly-placed table and came to relieve me of mine—including the goddamn pen. Then he moved back towards me and took my face in his hands. As he leaned down to kiss me, I closed my eyes and slid my arms around his waist, relaxing into him.

Sliding my hands onto his buttocks, I pulled him to me, feeling his erection already straining against his jeans. I moaned into his mouth, and the noise seemed to flip a switch in us both. Our movements went from sensual to frenzied in a millisecond.

Declan picked me up, then walked over to a rug on the floor and unceremoniously deposited me onto it. Tugging off his T-shirt, he revealed a body that many a younger man would have been jealous of. He didn't have a six-pack or pecs of steel, but he was toned and—I reached up to find out for myself—hard. He had a dusting of fine hair, and a treasure trail that led enticingly to his crown jewels.

I grinned. "Come on then, off with the rest of them."

Without missing a beat, he replied, "I will if you will."

We raced to strip. I, for one, was now desperate to have him inside me. Our initial misgivings out of the way, we both knew what we wanted. And that was each other.

Once we were naked, Declan rooted in the pocket of his discarded jeans and produced a condom, which he rolled on without fuss.

"Later," he murmured, straddling me, "I'm going to make love to you properly, the way you deserve." He nudged my knees apart and positioned his thick cock at my entrance. "But right now, I've just got to have you."

As he slid home, I wrapped my legs around his back. Looping my arms around his neck, I pulled him closer until we were skin to skin from head to, well, crotch. I was wet enough that he penetrated me effortlessly and we both groaned at the incredible sensation.

That was nothing, though. When Declan started to rotate his hips, crushing his pubic bone against my clit, I dug my nails into his shoulders in ecstasy. His movement, coupled with the friction against my G-spot, drove me wild. If this was *not* making love to me properly, I couldn't wait to see what was.

He rocked into me deeply but slowly, and his intense eye contact made the whole thing ten times more erotic and arousing. This was a guy who really knew how to seduce and please a woman. He leaned down to kiss me, sucking gently on my bottom lip before slipping his tongue into my mouth. I melted all over again. The combination of him being so damn attractive, so sexually talented, and the fact we were fucking on his floor was overwhelming. I just couldn't get enough.

I pulled away from our kiss only to whisper, "Please, Declan, make me come. I can't wait any longer. You're driving me crazy."

The dimples and the wrinkles around his eyes reappeared as he murmured back, "I'm glad to hear it. I'm also not one to deny a lady."

With that, he kissed me again, then raised himself up on his arms and began to fuck me in earnest. I took the opportunity to look at him as he coaxed my body towards the dizzying heights of orgasm. I saw glimpses of his thick cock as it penetrated me. It glistened with my juices. The muscles of his torso and arms flexed, and I dropped my hands from around his neck to grip his biceps. I sucked in a deep breath and smiled, enjoying the feel of the solid muscles beneath my fingers. I'd always been attracted to strong men, knowing how their power often equated to sexual dynamite. Unfortunately, though, so many of them were also self-centred gym freaks with not much between the ears. This was clearly not the case with Declan, and for that I was incredibly grateful.

Soon, all thoughts flew from my head except for one: *I'm going to come!*

I squeezed my eyes closed as I was overtaken by the immense pressure which signalled the onset of my orgasm. Then, following a couple more strokes of Declan's pubic bone to my clit, the dam broke. I screamed his name as I came, gushing all over his cock and clinging so tightly to his biceps I'd probably leave marks.

Declan came shortly afterwards in a series of jerky thrusts, grunts, and a moan that thrilled me all over again. I opened my eyes in time to catch his grin before he rolled off me. He bid me wait a few seconds while he got rid of the condom, then he came back, settled down next to me and pulled me into his arms.

It was then, as we lay together, basking in the afterglow of our respective orgasms that I realised something. I still didn't know how old he was. And what was more, I didn't care. All I knew was that I'd definitely be back to see the bookcases. And lots more besides.

I'm Tied Up Right Now

Nicole pushed the key into the door of hers and Steve's house and let herself in. "Hey, babe, I'm home!"

His response was muffled. "Hi, babe. I'm in here."

She sighed. Even without asking, she knew where "here" was. The damn office. Or, more accurately, the spare room that Steve had turned into a computer geek's wet dream. She'd accepted, when they'd moved in, that it would take a while for him to get things set up. It was his home office, so it had to be right. But unfortunately, it had turned into a job that was never finished. Everything was functioning, apparently, but he always seemed to be in there, replacing motherboards and hard drives, adding more RAM—she barely saw him.

After passing through to the kitchen, she put her bag down on the worktop and flicked on the kettle. "You want a coffee?" she shouted.

"I can't hear you, babe," came the reply. "I'm a little tied up right now."

I'll give you fucking tied up right now. She'd been a computer widow for months and was fed up of it. Marching through the house and into the spare room, she prepared to let him have it. But she soon discovered that even now, she'd be letting rip to his back. He was under the desk, just his back, bottom, legs and feet visible, and he hadn't a damn clue she was there.

"I said, do you want a coffee?" she yelled at the top of her voice, getting an immense feeling of satisfaction when Steve jumped out of his skin and smacked his head on the underside of the desk.

He emerged slowly, then turned and stood, rubbing his head. "Ow. There's no need to be like that. That bloody hurt my head, that did. I might have a concussion now."

She rolled her eyes. "Of course you haven't got a fucking concussion. And it serves you right, anyway. I'm sick and tired of playing second fiddle to all this." She gestured to the leads and components scattered everywhere, then picked up a yellow cable and waved it around for good measure.

"Hey, watch that! It's new."

"Shut up. It's a bloody cable, not a hard drive."

"You could still damage it."

She huffed out a breath, rage building inside her until it overflowed and forced her to do something about it. Moving over to him, she reached up and slapped his face, hard. While he was still reeling from the shock, she moved behind him and tied his hands together behind his back using the yellow cable.

"W-what are you doing?" Steve sounded genuinely worried, but she knew better. They'd played this game before.

"Sit down and shut up."

"There's nowhere to sit." It was true—he'd moved the chair out of the room as it was in the way of all his junk.

"Then sit on the fucking floor," she barked, a bolt of twisted pleasure coursing through her as he did as he was told.

She placed her high-heel-shod feet either side of his thighs, so her crotch was in front of his face. Then, not quite knowing what she was doing, or why, she pulled up her skirt and yanked her thong to one side. "Lick me," she demanded.

She expected confusion, surprise, refusal... anything that befitted the craziness of what was taking place. But she got none of those things, instead moaning and quickly locking her knees to take her weight as Steve's tongue slipped between her pussy lips.

It had been so long since he'd paid her any attention at all, let alone sexual attention, that she'd forgotten what it was like. But as his talented tongue caressed her slit, causing her juices to flow rapidly, the memories came back. Tangling her fingers into his hair, she rocked against his face, letting the delicious sensations wash over her. Her arousal grew so much that all she really wanted was to come. So she treated Steve like a sex toy, rubbing off against his lips and tongue, pulling him more tightly to her and using him to get her off.

Whether it was the physical sensations or the anger or the situation, she didn't know. But her orgasm hit fast and hard, and she hung more tightly onto Steve's hair to steady herself, taking extra pleasure from the fact that his scalp was probably on fire by now. Her throat was hoarse as she yelled her ecstasy at the ceiling, and it was all she could do not to crumple onto Steve's lap as her climax rendered her limbs jellylike. She managed to keep it together, riding it out until she eventually felt able to move.

Then she stepped away from her husband and pulled her knickers and skirt back into place. Glancing at him, she saw he looked as shell-shocked as she felt. He wriggled, then gave a small smile. "You gonna let me out of this?"

She raised an eyebrow, then lifted her foot and pushed it against his chest until he fell backwards onto the floor. "No, I'm not.

Not yet. I'm going to make a fucking coffee."

With that, she sashayed back out of the room and into the kitchen, thinking perhaps all those leads and cables weren't so bad, after all. They'd certainly come in handy to remind her husband of what he was missing out on while he tinkered with his stupid gadgets. She had a feeling he'd be more attentive in future, too.

Off the Beaten Track

Libby huffed and puffed as she made her way up the steep slope leading to the rear exit of the hotel complex. She swore the builders had had secret CCTV cameras installed so they could watch people suffer their poor planning for years to come. At least it was early. Had it been lunchtime, she'd surely have passed out with the heat.

Ah well, Libby thought as she finally reached the road, *it'll be worth it. This trip is going to be amazing.*

As she stood on the mercifully flat pavement and got her breath back, a thought niggled at her. Nobody else was here. Panicking, Libby wrenched open her bag and pulled out her paperwork. She examined it. A glance at her watch confirmed she had both the right date *and* time. So where was everyone? She was ten minutes early, but surely the others should be here by now? She looked down the slope she'd just ascended and frowned. No one else was heading in her direction.

Fuck. Perhaps they were all here earlier and they've gone without me!

The rumble of an engine snapped her attention to the road. A jeep trundled towards her. She waited hopefully as the driver pulled the vehicle up beside where she stood and reached into the passenger seat.

The man retrieved a clipboard and peered at it for a moment. Then he looked at her. "You are Libby Strong?"

She nodded.

The man grinned widely, revealing dimples in both cheeks,

and hopped out of the jeep. He walked around the vehicle, then approached her and held out a hand. "I am Demetrio. Your guide for the day."

Libby took his hand and shook it. It was warm and strong. Much like the rest of him, she suspected, giving him a subtle once over. He was tall, with black curly hair to his shoulders, luscious brown eyes, and olive skin. A white T-shirt bearing the holiday company's logo covered his top half—though without obscuring his impressive biceps—and he wore longish tan-coloured shorts on the bottom. A pair of non-descript white-ish trainers and faded red cap completed his outfit.

"I'm Libby," she said, then cringed inwardly as she remembered he already knew her name. Oh well, she was just being polite. "Pleased to meet you."

They broke off the handshake and Demetrio smiled again, then moved to the passenger side of the jeep and pulled open the door. "Please," he said, gesturing she should get in.

Libby did as she was told, but couldn't help asking the burning question. "Where is everyone else?"

Demetrio waited until she was safely in the passenger seat, then closed the door and made his way to the driver's side. He got in, then turned to her with a shrug. "There is nobody else. You are only person on this trip. You get best views!"

He laughed, the flash of white teeth against olive skin resulting in an unexpected jolt in Libby's nether regions. She studied his profile for a few seconds, then grudgingly admitted to herself that Demetrio was, in fact, very attractive. Despite the fact she was a red-blooded woman, she rarely paid attention to such things.

Like most people, she'd come on holiday to recharge her batteries. Unlike most people, she'd been practically forced into it. Libby was somewhat of a workaholic, which left her little time for anything else. This had cost her her last relationship. The long working hours, frequent rain checks on their dates, and her lack of interest in any kind of affection, let alone sex, had finally caused James to walk away.

Libby had barely noticed. She'd just carried on working, and working… until her friends and family had finally intervened. They'd booked the holiday to Portugal, arranged with her boss for her to have the time off, and basically given her little choice but to go.

Libby hadn't been impressed. "I'll sleep when I'm dead," she'd quipped.

But she'd been both outnumbered and outmanoeuvred, and so here she was.

Consoling herself with the fact she could at least do some sightseeing—she wasn't the lie-by-the-pool-and-sunbathe type— Libby had booked the day-long jeep tour so she could go further afield than the resort she was staying in. She could have hired a car, but she didn't fancy taking off on her own. She'd seen the shit heaps the hire companies were using, and there was no way she was going to risk breaking down in a strange place, by herself. So a jeep tour it was.

Apparently everyone else holidaying in the area preferred the lying-by-the-pool option. At least it explained how Demetrio had known her name. She was the only one on the list!

She frowned. "Demetrio," she said, interrupting him as he moved to start the jeep, "if I'm the only person on the trip, why wasn't it cancelled? Surely it's not worth it?"

She didn't want it to be cancelled, of course, but curiosity wouldn't let her keep quiet.

Demetrio turned to her. "It does not matter. If I do not make the trip, I do not get paid. So here I am."

Libby couldn't argue with that logic, so she said nothing and gave Demetrio a grateful smile. "Well, I'm glad you are. I'm looking forward to seeing some of the country."

She reached for her seatbelt and fastened it around her, causing Demetrio to hesitate in starting the jeep once more.

"Ah, yes," he said, mimicking her actions, "my seatbelt. I do not normally bother."

Libby opened her mouth to tell him why he should always wear a seatbelt, then promptly closed it again as he smiled and shrugged, then finally fired up the engine. Things here were much more relaxed.

The jeep's engine roared as Demetrio pressed the accelerator pedal a little too enthusiastically, and they were away. Libby's adventure had begun.

As they moved away from the streets bordered by tall buildings and onto the open road, the sun's rays found them. Warmth caressed Libby's body. She gave a satisfied sigh, let her head loll back against the seat, and closed her eyes.

Demetrio's voice broke the silence. "You are tired, Libby?"

She snapped back upright and looked at him. "No, just…
happy."

As the word came out of her mouth, Libby was surprised to
realise just how much she meant it. She didn't think she'd been
*un*happy before. She loved her work, so all the hours she put in were
no real hardship, but it wasn't until now, when she was doing
something completely different, that she realised what she'd been
missing out on. *Life.* She'd been the girl who "works hard and plays
hard," but had forgotten the play part.

Well, it was time to put a stop to that. She smiled and looked
out at the world racing by. The jeep's open windows and roof were
playing havoc with her hair, but for once, she didn't care. She was
on holiday.

They continued their journey in silence for a while. Soon
they left the urban area and motored onto a dual carriageway which
led them inland. Libby gasped, then quickly rooted around in her bag
to retrieve her camera. Once she had it ready, she didn't know what
to take photographs of first—the sea glittering in the sunlight behind
them, the rolling hills they were heading towards, or all of the beauty
in between. She clicked madly and got them all in turn, then clicked
some more. Luckily, she had tons of space on the digital camera's
memory card. If this, the first leg of their trip, was anything to go by,
she'd be taking lots of photos today.

When Demetrio touched her on the shoulder, she jumped and
turned to face him, her hair flying in front of her face in the process.
When she eventually got it under control, Demetrio glanced at her
and grinned, his dimples showing again. With his curls trapped

beneath the cap, he wasn't experiencing the hair issues Libby was. He clearly knew better.

"Sorry," he shouted over the din of the rushing wind, "I wanted to show you something. Up there."

He glanced in his mirrors to make sure nobody was following close behind them, then slowed the jeep down. Pointing up the hillside they were heading towards, he yelled, "We are going up there."

Libby followed the line of his finger. She couldn't see anything in particular, just a sea of dark green covering the hills, with the occasional building peeking out here and there. Not wanting to appear foolish, Libby said, loudly enough to be heard over the noise, "I can't wait."

Just then, the jeep hit a bump in the road. The momentum rocked Libby closer to Demetrio, and she accidentally brushed against his arm. Libby immediately wrenched herself back to her side of the car like she'd been burned. Then she scolded herself. Why on earth was she behaving like a schoolgirl because she'd accidentally bumped into Demetrio's arm? His very *muscular* arm. She peeked at him. He really did have the most delicious biceps…

He didn't seem any worse off for their mishap, merely pushing the accelerator harder to get them back up to speed. He probably hadn't even noticed. Shaking her head, Libby mentally cursed herself. Why was he making her feel this way? *Probably because you need to get laid, girl,* said a little devil inside her head. *And you could do much worse.*

It was true. Demetrio was definitely a hottie. Examining him out of the corner of her eye, she glanced at his hands upon the wheel. More specifically, his left hand. No wedding ring. Of course that didn't mean he didn't have a girlfriend, but she could still hope.

As she forced her attention back to the road, she noticed they were almost right up to the hills. Sure enough, seconds later, Demetrio indicated and steered the jeep down the next exit slip road. After negotiating a roundabout, they headed into a village, which caused Libby to grab her camera and start taking photographs again.

One pretty village led to the next, the zigzagging roads carrying them up the hillside. Libby alternately marvelled at the scenery and at Demetrio, depending on which way her head was turned.

Demetrio turned to Libby. "Hold tight to your camera now. We are heading onto bumpy roads."

Libby could have sworn his gaze briefly flicked to her breasts then, as if thinking how they'd bounce on the bumpy roads he'd just mentioned. But he said nothing else, simply taking a turn up a track. The tarmac quickly tailed off and turned into rocks and dirt.

By the time they reached a cluster of buildings and drew to a stop, Libby was glad they'd been travelling in a 4x4. Demetrio hadn't been kidding about the bumps. It had been kind of fun actually, but she was glad of the respite, however brief.

She was still disentangling herself from the seatbelt and grabbing her bag when Demetrio appeared at her door and opened it.

Smiling, Libby got herself straightened out, then took the proffered hand and stepped down from the jeep as gracefully as possible. She was glad she'd worn shorts and not a skirt—not to mention sensible shoes. She may not exactly be in sex-kitten attire, but she wouldn't be tripping over her flip flops or flashing her knickers any time soon. "Thank you."

When she was safely out of the jeep, Libby pulled the strap of her bag over her head so she had both hands free to use her camera. As she glanced back at Demetrio, she had second thoughts about flashing her knickers. The way he was looking at her made her think that perhaps the lustful thoughts she was experiencing weren't one sided. Suddenly, he seemed to realise she was looking at him, and snapped out of it. He beamed. "Come. This is first stop off. There are bathrooms here, also, if you need."

She did need. He showed her where they were, then waited outside.

"Ready?" he asked when she emerged.

Giving a nod and a smile, she followed him as he headed through a gap between two buildings into what looked like a courtyard of sorts. She took the opportunity to admire the way his arse looked in his shorts. They weren't particularly tight, but nevertheless, the view was very pleasant indeed.

What happened next was somewhat of a blur. As they entered the courtyard, a cacophony began. A dog rushed out from somewhere and began yapping and making a big fuss of Demetrio—a fuss he gladly returned—then an old woman followed, grabbing Demetrio's face between her hands and placing a kiss on each of his cheeks before unleashing a torrent of Portuguese Libby couldn't even begin to translate. All she could surmise was that both the dog and the woman were pleased to see Demetrio—and she didn't need verbal language for that. In this case, body language spoke volumes.

A rapid conversation took place between Demetrio and the woman. The woman then approached Libby and took her hand. "Forgive me," she said, her English even more heavily accented than Demetrio's. "I am Telma. Please, come try our firewater."

With that, she turned and shuffled through the courtyard, the dog at her side, without waiting to see if Demetrio and Libby followed.

Libby was confused. *This wasn't on the itinerary. Or was it?* It had mentioned trying local produce.

They walked towards another set of buildings. A man, who Libby suspected was Telma's husband, came out. He also made a big fuss of Demetrio, unleashing a rapid torrent of Portuguese and indulging in some hearty back-slapping.

That done, he turned to Libby with a toothy grin. "Hello. I am Carlos. Very nice to meet you." Instead of shaking her hand, he thrust a shot glass full of clear liquid into her hand. "Is firewater. We make here. You try."

Libby looked to Demetrio for reassurance, but he merely smiled and made a drinking motion with his hand.

"Aren't you having any?"

He laughed and shook his head emphatically. "No! I must drive. Go on, you try. All at once."

Resisting the temptation to sniff the liquid before drinking it, she closed her eyes and knocked it back in one go. Opening her eyes again and smiling triumphantly at the three expectant faces, she wondered why it was called firewater. She was just about to ask when the answer hit her. The liquid burned a trail of fire down her throat, all the way into her gut.

Her face must have expressed her surprise and discomfort as the three Portuguese clapped and laughed, though not in a spiteful way.

Demetrio said, "The firewater is for sale. You want to buy?"

There was a twinkle in his eye. He was teasing her.

She shook her head. "I-I don't think so. Thank you."

"Come," he said, unperturbed, "we must be on our way."

A torrent of Portuguese ensued as he said his goodbyes to the old couple, who waved at her. She waved back, thanked them for their hospitality, then followed Demetrio to the jeep, realising about halfway there she was actually a little drunk. How was that even possible from a tiny shot glass of the stuff?

Demetrio looked over his shoulder at her, then smiled as he noted her expression. He stopped and waited, holding his arm out. She took it, and as their bodies touched, the heat that had been burning in her throat and stomach seemed to radiate throughout her entire body, eventually pooling in her groin. Fuck, she was horny.

She looked up at him as they reached the jeep, grinning widely.

He laughed softly and helped her back into her seat. After getting into the driver's side, he reached into the rear of the vehicle and grabbed a bottle of water. He opened it and passed it to Libby, who accepted it gratefully. She took several large gulps, slowly starting to feel more like herself, except for the heat between her legs. That didn't seem to go away.

"Okay?" Demetrio asked, raising one eyebrow. "The firewater is strong, yes?"

She nodded, grinning sheepishly.

"Are you ready to go? You have your camera?"

Nodding again, Libby put on her seatbelt and relaxed as Demetrio steered them back onto the dirt track. Rather than returning to the main road, he took them further along the track, deeper into the countryside. The land on either side of the track gave way to orange groves, and just as Libby delightedly noticed the big, fat fruits hanging from the branches, she caught their scent.

She dragged in deep breaths, enjoying the divine smell. The fragrance of a single orange was nice, but this was something else. She took photos as they drove along the winding track, beaming until her face almost hurt. *God, I feel like I'm on top of the world.* She had no idea if it was the firewater, the sun, the scenery, or what. But she liked it.

A sudden dip in the track pulled her attention back to her more immediate surroundings. Demetrio had both hands tightly on the wheel and was concentrating intently. She soon realised why as the slope grew steeper and they trundled onto shingle. They'd emerged into some kind of clearing, which was full of small rocks and had a stream running into it at one end.

Demetrio pulled the jeep as close to the stream as he dared and turned off the engine. "Well," he said, turning to Libby with a grin, "what do you think? You are having fun?"

Libby couldn't help but smile back. His happiness was infectious. "I am having fun, yes. Thank you, Demetrio."

"I am pleased. Would you like something to eat?"

Libby frowned and looked at her watch. It was lunchtime. She'd had no idea. *What is it they say? 'Time flies when you're having fun'.* Undoing her seatbelt, she voiced her agreement.

Demetrio undid his own seatbelt and scrambled from the vehicle, then leaned into the back of it.

She got out of the jeep and walked around to where Demetrio was retrieving sandwiches and drinks from a cool box. "Demetrio," she said softly.

He turned and looked at her, a package of sandwiches in each hand. He offered one to her.

She shook her head. "Demetrio," she repeated, hardly knowing where her sudden boldness was coming from, "do you have a girlfriend?"

He moved his head slowly from side to side, clearly confused.

"Do you like me?" She gestured at her body, making her intentions clear.

He gulped and put the sandwiches back in the cool box. "I-I think you are very beautiful."

Libby moved right in front of Demetrio and looked up at him. "Would you…" she forced herself to continue before she lost her nerve, "like to make love?"

Rather than responding verbally, he took off his cap and tossed it into the back of the jeep. Then he grabbed Libby's hand and pulled her around the vehicle, to the side away from the track. He pushed her up against the side of the jeep, took her face in his hands, and kissed her. It was gentle, yet passionate, and a tingle spread through Libby's body which had nothing to do with the alcohol she'd consumed. This was lust, pure and simple.

Reaching up and bunching his soft hair in one hand, Libby wrapped the other arm around his back and pulled Demetrio closer, so his body pressed to hers, trapping her between him and the jeep. She quickly discovered he was just as aroused as she was; his erection pressed against her stomach. Closing her eyes as they deepened the kiss, she moaned. Demetrio pressed his hard cock more forcefully against her.

Twisting her face away, Libby gasped. Fuck the foreplay, she wanted him now. "Demetrio. Pass me my bag."

He pulled away from her, then reached into the vehicle and retrieved the bag. He handed it to her wordlessly and watched, his breathing heavy, as she unearthed a condom from its depths with a cry of triumph.

She dropped the bag at her feet, then reached out and grabbed the waistband of Demetrio's shorts, dragging him in for another toe-curling kiss. After a minute or two, she breathlessly pushed him away again.

Before he had chance to react, Libby undid the condom wrapper, tossed it into her bag and said, "Pull down your shorts."

The second it was revealed, Libby took stock of his erection. Liquid soaked her knickers. *Fuck*, it looked good—long, thick, and raring to go. She handed him the condom, then wriggled out of her own shorts and thong as he rolled it on. Once they were both ready, their eyes met and there was no hesitation. They'd gone way past that.

Demetrio closed the gap between them, pressed a kiss to her lips, then reached down to lift one of her legs. He bent at the knees and used his free hand to position his cock at her entrance. She tilted her hips towards him, and he drove deep inside her.

Libby let out a yell and dug her fingernails into his shoulders as her pussy stretched around his thick shaft. She was so wet that it didn't hurt, exactly, but it had been a while. Once he was inside her balls-deep, he looked her in the eye, a question there. She gave a nod. *Hell yeah, I want you to fuck me.*

With her leg hooked over one arm, he braced himself against the jeep with the other and began to fuck her for all he was worth. She clung to him, gasping and wailing as delicious feelings overtook her. She was being pounded against the sun-warmed metal at her back, but she couldn't give a shit. God, she hoped nobody came down that track any time soon, because there was no way they'd be able to stop. They were entirely lost to lust, to passion.

She moved one of her hands from his shoulder and placed it on his firm arse, then used it to pull him harder into her. He took the hint and picked up his pace further, causing her orgasm to slam into her with a force that took her breath away. She couldn't make a sound as her muscles tensed and her cunt squeezed Demetrio's cock in an iron grip.

Demetrio had no such problem. He grunted and spat out a few words of Portuguese, then stilled as his own climax hit.

Libby finally found her voice and gasped as Demetrio's cock twitched powerfully inside her, emptying his balls into the condom.

They clung to each other, panting as they rode out their respective orgasms and drifted into afterglow.

A little while later, they disentangled and Libby heard the snap of rubber as Demetrio turned away from her and removed the condom. She grinned, the after-effects of spectacular sex making her clumsy as she fumbled with her clothes.

As they tumbled simultaneously into the jeep several minutes later, they shared a smile.

Still buzzing, Libby said, "I think I'll have that food now, Demetrio. I've worked up *quite* an appetite."

His broad grin told her her comment hadn't been lost in translation, and as she watched his lean body reach over into the back of the jeep to retrieve their delayed lunch, she grinned devilishly.

Orange groves and firewater be damned. He *is definitely the highlight of this trip.*

Spa Daze

Claire skulked out of the changing rooms. She knew everyone else was wearing swimwear too, but it didn't make her any less self-conscious. Casting her eyes between the swimming pool and the unoccupied hot tub, she made her decision and scurried to the latter, dumping her towelling robe on a lounger along the way.

Sinking into the furiously bubbling water, Claire already felt more relaxed. She'd been having a hard time of it lately and had treated herself to a day at a spa so she could have some 'me-time.' No mobile phones, no computers, no distractions. Far from feeling cut off, Claire loved it. If anyone needed her, tough. It was her day and she was damn well going to enjoy it.

She moved her arms and legs gently about in the tub, experimenting with different positions. If she stretched her legs just so, a jet blasted bubbles right between her wriggling toes. Bliss.

The force of the numerous jets hitting her body shifted her bottom along the seat a little. However, when Claire settled back down, she found she didn't mind at all.

Her new position meant a stream of bubbles was directed right between her legs. Claire idly scissored them open and closed a few times, the picture of innocence to anyone who may have happened across her. As it was, the place was quiet. Two older women were doing slow laps in the pool, chatting to each other and paying her no heed. The jacuzzi was set above the pool in any case, so all they'd see if they looked in her direction was her head over the mosaic-tiled wall.

Claire draped her arms over the side of the tub and opened

her legs. The jet was so strong that it felt as if she was naked down there. The bubbles pummelled and caressed her pussy. Even with the constant sensation of the water, Claire felt blood flowing to the juncture of her thighs. Her labia started to swell and her clit throbbed.

Despite knowing no one could possibly see what she was doing, Claire glanced around again to make sure nobody was looking in her direction. The coast was clear. Spreading her legs wider, she succumbed to the jacuzzi's relentless stimulation. Leaning her head back, Claire closed her eyes, every inch the relaxed spa customer. If only they knew.

Using her arms to shift her body just a tiny bit, Claire aimed the jet where she needed it most. Soon her pussy fluttered, the beginnings of orgasm creeping over her. A few more seconds of direct contact was all it took. Squeezing her eyes even more tightly shut, she gritted her teeth and pressed her lips together hard as her climax tore through her body. A noise escaped her throat, but was lost in the noise of the bubbling tub.

Claire slumped in the seat, breathing hard. As she started to come back to herself, she cracked open her lids, ready to let the world back in.

The most inviting green eyes she'd ever seen were peering back at her.

Startled, Claire's heart leapt and she squeaked, "You made me jump!"

Standing at the edge of the jacuzzi was a very amused young man. Dressed in the spa's staff uniform of white shorts and navy T-shirt, he was every inch the health and wellbeing guru. He had a tanned body that he clearly looked after, and tousled blonde hair. He could have walked off Bondi Beach. Claire was suddenly very aware of her pale, decidedly un-toned body.

"Sorry. I was just walking past and you looked like you were in pain. I thought you had cramp or something."

"Uh…" She thought fast. "Yeah. In my leg. It's okay now, though."

He wrinkled his nose thoughtfully. "I think I should probably look at it. If the muscle isn't properly relaxed, the pain could come back. I'm a sports masseuse, by the way. Jackson."

Claire couldn't see any way of refusing without appearing rude. She wasn't sure she wanted to, to be honest. After all, it wasn't every day an extremely sexy sports masseuse offered to put his hands on her leg, or anywhere else for that matter.

"Okay, if you're sure. Would you mind passing me my robe? It's on the nearest lounger."

Jackson walked to the lounger, and Claire nodded when he pointed to make sure he'd got the right one. He scooped it up and returned to the side of the tub, then held out the robe and waited while she got into it. Claire snatched the sides together and quickly tied the belt around her waist, not wanting her body on display for any longer than necessary. "Thank you."

"No worries." He grinned. "All part of the service. Follow me."

Jackson set off towards the changing rooms. Claire wondered what on earth he was up to, when she remembered there was a unisex area just before the corridors forked off in opposite directions. Sure enough, he headed into a communal area with a water fountain, showers, some seating, and the sauna and steam rooms.

Claire was just settling into one of the chairs when Jackson whipped off his T-shirt and started folding it. Her jaw all but hit the floor. He was facing away from her, and as much as she wanted to see the front view, the back view was pretty damn delicious. He had broad, muscular shoulders, and biceps to die for. There was a tattoo on his right shoulder blade and another circling his left arm. As she gawped, Jackson hooked his thumbs into the waistband of his shorts and kicked off his flip flops, then shoved the shorts down.

She almost had a coronary until she realised he was wearing swimming trunks underneath. Of course he was. In case he had to leap into the pool to save someone. Claire herself was in danger of drowning—in her own drool.

The shorts dropped to his ankles. When he bent to pick them up, Claire bit her lip hard to keep from making a noise. If she had, it would have been something like "Mmmmmffff!"

His arse was to die for just as much as his biceps—if not more so.

Before her mind had chance to disappear too far into the gutter, Jackson walked to the steam room door, opened it, and said, "You coming then?"

Claire nodded dumbly. She took off her robe and put it on a chair, then followed him in to the steam room and closed the door behind her. Immediately, she was enveloped in a warm, steamy embrace and she paused for a moment to let her eyes adjust to the dimly-lit room. Once she was confident she could see where she was going, she moved to the wooden platforms used for seating, and went to perch on the one at right angles to where Jackson was sitting.

Before she could sit down he said, "What are you doing? How am I meant to massage your calf muscle from there?"

What with all the distraction of Jackson taking his clothes off and asking her to join him in a steam room, Claire had completely forgotten about the massage for her non-existent cramp. Chastised, she moved to the end of Jackson's bench and gingerly lowered herself onto the hot wood, then twisted to face him. She couldn't remember telling him which leg it was, so she mentally crossed her fingers she hadn't, and stretched out her right leg towards him.

He gently took her ankle and placed her foot in his lap. Claire was painfully aware of how close it was to his groin. Then he put his hands on her calf muscle and started to manipulate it. After that, Claire wasn't aware of much else. Her natural reaction was to make lots of "ooh" and "ahh" noises as he massaged her, but she kept her mouth shut for fear of sounding like a porn star.

As Jackson's talented hands swept over her skin and kneaded at her muscles, she started to sweat. She'd always preferred steam rooms over saunas as the heat wasn't so dry and extreme. But what with there being an incredibly attractive man touching her and still feeling horny after her hot tub orgasm, Claire was really feeling the heat.

A droplet of sweat ran down her spine. She shuddered, all her hairs standing on end.

"You all right?" Jackson asked, a frown marring his perfect face.

She gave a tight smile. "Yes, I'm fine. Just starting to feel the heat, that's all."

He smiled. Damp hair flopped around his face and his skin glowed with a sheen of sweat. He glanced at Claire's chest, then away. She swore she could see a tiny smirk on his face. Looking down, she realised why. Her nipples were totally giving the game away. They were rock hard and pressing against her bikini top. Making the excuse she was cold was clearly not going to cut it. So she said nothing.

"Well," he said after a few minutes of silence, releasing her leg, "there doesn't appear to be any tension in the muscle now. You shouldn't have any more trouble with it."

Claire pulled her "bad" leg back, then tucked both of them up and leaned her chin on her knees. "Thank you, that was lovely."

"No problem. Though it wasn't meant to be lovely; it's supposed to release tension."

"I know," she said, grateful she was already so hot she was red-faced, hiding her embarrassment, "but massage is always lovely. Especially from…" what she'd been about to say was 'you,' but she quickly corrected herself, "a professional."

Realising she'd inadvertently divulged details of her past sex life, she looked away and stared intently at her toes.

When she dragged her gaze back up, Jackson was still looking at her. She forced herself to maintain eye contact and, although it hardly seemed possible, the temperature in the room appeared to rise a few more degrees. Despite the damp atmosphere, her mouth and throat went dry.

"Well, I'm glad you enjoyed it," Jackson said, shuffling up and closing the gap between them. "You seem to be enjoying yourself rather a lot today, don't you?"

As she opened her mouth to respond, she clocked his lascivious expression.

Fuck. He knew.

As her brain floundered around for some kind of excuse, he added, "You're not the first person to get off in that hot tub, you know."

Claire gaped. Not very attractive, but Jackson didn't seem to care. He moved closer still and put a finger beneath her jaw, then pushed her mouth closed.

"I knew what you were doing." Now he was so close her toes almost touched the side of his leg. "And it was really hot. See what you've done to me?"

He grabbed her wrist and placed her hand on his crotch. His cock was rock hard. The knowledge made Claire even hornier, and a trickle of juice seeped from her pussy. The fact she hadn't snatched her hand away was apparently all the invitation Jackson needed. He slipped his hand between her legs, pulled aside the material covering her pussy, and dipped his fingers into her slit.

"Well," he said, stroking up and down her juice-slicked vulva, "somebody is *very* horny today, aren't they?"

Claire pressed her hand harder against his cock by way of response. She made small circles and felt his shaft twitch beneath her fingers. He retaliated by pushing two fingers inside her and zoning in on her G-spot. After curling his thumb up to her clit, he began to finger-fuck her in earnest, making her writhe on the bench.

Jackson's pleasure was all but forgotten as Claire felt her orgasm approach. The craziness of the situation, Jackson's pure, unadulterated sex appeal, and the possibility of being caught ramped up her arousal. Before long, she was biting her own hand to keep from screaming as she bucked against his fingers, riding out her sweaty climax.

As the tremors slowed, Jackson removed his hand and put it to his mouth. He sucked a finger between those pouty lips and licked up all her juices, then repeated with the other soaked digit.

Still feeling a little wrung out from her orgasm, Claire smiled and moved ninety degrees on the seat. Then she dipped a hand inside his trunks and released his cock. It was damp with perspiration. Eager to return the favour, she wrapped her fingers around his shaft, and began to stroke up and down, squeezing lightly. Jackson gasped, but any further sound was swallowed as Claire covered his lips with hers.

Claire's pussy grew wetter still as Jackson's tongue thrust inside her mouth. He cupped the back of her neck and pulled her tighter to him, deepening the already sensual kiss. She moaned, and felt Jackson's thick cock leap beneath her fingers in response. Tightening her grip, Claire masturbated him more swiftly, enjoying the feeling of power as his kisses became more frenzied.

Soon, he pulled back a little, only to rest his forehead against hers. Looking down, she saw him bite his lip as his cock began to spurt its release. He grunted as semen shot out, again and again, hitting his abdomen and coating Claire's hand.

With a sigh of satisfaction, Jackson gave Claire a quick kiss, then tucked his cock back into his trunks, probably aware someone could arrive at any moment. "Hey," he said thickly, giving her a wicked grin, "you wanna go and continue your massage somewhere more private?"

"Can't think of anything I'd like more."

With that, they scrambled to leave, giggling like naughty schoolchildren.

It crossed Claire's mind she was behaving a little sluttishly. But she didn't care; nobody had to know. It was her sweaty little secret and she was going to enjoy it. Plus she *had* come here for some 'me-time'. And what could possibly be more indulgent than sex with a gorgeous sports masseuse?

Raising the Bar

The first restaurant I walk into has an opening. I can hardly believe my luck when they offer me the job on the spot. Even more so when I'm introduced to my colleagues. I've had so many different jobs so far on my gap year that I don't get first day jitters any more. But when my gaze meets the most gorgeous pair of brown eyes I've ever seen, I do more than jitter. My stomach flip-flops, and I stammer, blush, mumble something, and swiftly move on to the next introduction. I have no idea if anyone's noticed my weird behaviour, but to be honest I'm so distracted by the sudden heat between my legs that the thought leaves my head pretty quickly.

Besides, I have much more interesting things to think about. Like Luciano. The brown-haired, brown-eyed, brown-skinned sex god. He's so hot he should come with a health warning. In actual fact, if I don't pay more attention to what I'm doing at work, he will actually be detrimental to my health.

I throw myself into work. To take my mind off those eyes; to take my mind off the man they belong to.

It's tough. I can't avoid him. If truth be told, I don't really want to. But as we pass each other in the restaurant for the umpteenth time and the sparks fly between us, I know my self-imposed man-fast won't last much longer. Despite my frequent travelling, I haven't met anyone quite like him before. Met anyone who's made me *feel* quite like he does. I suspect he's going to be trouble. So much for being footloose and fancy free during my gap year. If I fall for him, my itinerary is going to be screwed. I'll never want to leave.

My first shift passes in a blur of non-descript customers and searing eye contact. My pussy swells and my clit throbs, desperate for attention. It's all I can do to resist disappearing into the bathroom for a sneaky wank. Even better, I'd like to drag Luciano in there with me and ride him until his teeth rattle. Instead, I console myself with the fact that once I get back to my apartment, I can do whatever the hell I like.

I take a taxi back to my apartment rather than walking the dark, unfamiliar streets alone. It also means I can get there quicker and relieve the tension the sexy Spaniard has caused. When I arrive home, I jump out of the taxi and pay the driver as fast as possible, then rush inside and slam the door behind me. I heave a sigh of relief as I lock myself in.

I undress, then drop my clothes by the washing machine and head to the bathroom, desperate to get clean. It's not work that's made me feel dirty, though. The eye-fucking and flirting with Luciano have left me with a seriously wet pussy. The panties I've just discarded in front of the washing machine are sodden.

Stepping under the shower head, I relish the feel of the hot spray caressing my skin. I stand there for a few seconds, letting the heat and water relax me. The tension slips away and runs down the plughole. I grab the shampoo and give my hair a wash, digging my fingers into my scalp and massaging it. I feel better. Calmer. But by the time I've rinsed the suds, he's popped into my head again. Damn him.

I've known him less than twenty-four hours and already he's driving me crazy. How is that normal? I turn under the spray, close my eyes and aim my face towards the water, as if to wash my thoughts clean. Fat chance, they're positively filthy! I slump forward and rest my forehead against the tiled wall. The shower runs on, rivulets of water hitting my neck and shoulders; then running down my back and into my arse crack. It doesn't help to distract me from the ache between my thighs. I have to do something about it. Now.

I slip my fingers to where I need them most; dip into the hot and silky wetness. I circle my clit, gasping at how distended it is. And all this from some flirting! What the hell would happen if he actually touched me? I'd probably melt into a puddle at his feet.

After slicking juices over my sensitive nub, I stroke it in earnest. I squeeze my eyes shut; and images of Luciano swim through my head. Slipping into the shower behind me; his brown arm covering mine, moving my fingers out of the way. Dipping his own digits into my wetness, before bringing me off with a few short strokes, then plunging his cock into me from behind and fucking me until I scream myself hoarse and see stars.

Seconds later, my orgasm crashes through my body with a ferocity that shocks and excites me. I'm sincerely glad of the four walls surrounding me, otherwise I'd be in serious danger of falling. I slump against the cool tiles to catch my breath and regain the use of my limbs. I also make an attempt to shove away the erotic images in my head. I'm certain it won't work, but I try anyway.

With my libido temporarily sated, I wash and rinse my body, then shut off the shower. I hop out, towel dry my body and hair, and get ready for bed.

I sigh happily as I sink beneath the cool sheets. After my

delicious orgasm in the shower, I thought I'd be asleep before my head hit the pillow. But in actual fact, I'm still raring and ready to go. Horny on thoughts of Luciano, I resort to a heated session with my trusty rabbit on top speed before I finally fall asleep.

***

Ugh. Today I'm working a double shift. It's not ideal, but it does mean I will have accrued enough hours to get a whole day off this week. Luciano's not in until the evening shift, so at least I can work my lunchtime shift with little distraction. Apart from my salacious thoughts, of course.

The afternoon passes uneventfully and it's soon time for my break between shifts. I don't particularly want to wander around the town in my uniform, spending money on stuff I don't need, so I head to the staff room. Though it's a joke that management call it a staff room. It's like sitting in a large box room. I've got a magazine and a sandwich, and I settle myself at the table, leafing through the pages as I eat.

I manage to finish my sandwich and most of my drink before my peace is shattered. The door opens and *he* walks in. My heart thumps. He looks momentarily surprised to see me, then flashes me a smile which has me squirming in my seat.

"Hello, Kayleigh. You are early?" His accented English is cute and sexy at the same time.

I battle my blushes and reply, "No, I'm working a double shift today."

"I see. You look tired. You did not sleep well?"

His question is perfectly innocent, but somehow I feel as though he's looking inside my head and knows the precise reason I had trouble sleeping. I can't help it; heat rises up my cheeks and I duck my head, hoping he won't notice.

"Oh," he says, smiling, "You have a boyfriend!"

I want the ground to swallow me up. What's worse, having him think I'm tired because I've been shagging all night, or because I've been wanking? The rash part of my brain takes over. I shake my head. "No, I don't have a boyfriend."

His handsome face loses its amused expression, and he comes to sit next to me. Immediately, sweat breaks out on my palms. I have no idea if he can feel it too, but his proximity raises my temperature a few notches, and my fingers twitch, desperate to reach out and touch him. Electricity crackles between us and I fidget in my seat, when what I really want to do is climb into his lap and do unspeakable things to him.

I wait for him to say something, and eventually the tension gets to me. To stop myself pouncing on him and planting a kiss on his lips, I grab my drink. Or at least, that's what I intend to do. Instead, I manage to knock it over, covering him in the remainder of my Coke. He jumps up, rambling in rapid Spanish, and leaves the room before I have chance to apologise.

Seconds later, he returns with a cloth. He hands it to me. "You wipe. I change clothes."

With that he whips off his T-shirt, completely unabashed. I dab at the spill, watching him from the corner of my eye. He either can't see me looking, or doesn't care, because he's removed his jeans, too. He stands there in tight, black boxer shorts and little else, whilst he rifles around in his bag for his uniform. I bite my lip to suppress a lusty groan. God, he looks good enough to eat. Or, you know, fuck.

He turns around. I glance away quickly, but not before he's caught me staring.

"You were looking at me?"

My blush gives me away, making lies futile. I stare at the table.

"It is okay," he says, moving over to me and lifting my chin, "I look at you, too. You are beautiful."

As I start to mumble a protest, he covers my lips with his fingers. "Do you like me?"

I look into his chocolate-coloured eyes, powerless to do anything except nod. It's like he's got me under some kind of spell. A horny spell, perhaps.

He takes my hand. "I like you, too."

Then he kisses me. He tastes of coffee and chocolate. His almost-naked form presses against me, as does the unmistakable bulge of his cock. I abandon the cloth and respond to his kiss, slip my arms around him and appreciate the feel of his smooth, slim, and yet athletic body. I usually like my men big and beefy, capable of throwing me around in the bedroom, but there's just something about him, with his narrow hips and tight bottom which makes me tingle in all the right places.

Just as I begin to lose myself in his kiss, he pulls away. I open my mouth to protest, then shut it promptly when he slips to the door, flips the lock, and rejoins me. His erection has created a sizable tent in his underwear. My pussy throbs in response to the sight. I want him. He follows my gaze, smiles and shrugs, then kisses me again.

As he titillates me with his tongue, he slips a hand under my skirt, pushes the gusset of my knickers to one side and touches me. I'm already wet, and more juices begin to flow as Luciano expertly strokes my slippery folds and teases my clit. I tremble a little. All these weeks of abstinence and then he comes along. No wonder I'm so fucking horny. There's plenty to be said for masturbation, but it doesn't compare to the real thing. Especially not with him.

He pushes me gently backwards until I'm pressed against the wall. I gasp as his busy fingers suddenly leave my clit and enter me. He curls them and begins finger-fucking my cunt. Each thrust rubs against a sensitive place that I never noticed before, though I've read about it. He kisses me again, his tongue entwining sensuously with mine. I moan into his mouth as I feel a strange sensation in my pussy. It's totally incredible. The more he manipulates the spot, the more intense it feels, and soon he has to pull away from our kiss and clamp his free hand over my mouth to stifle my squeal as I squirt all over his hand.

Wow. So that's my G-spot, huh?

I pull in a shaky breath when he removes his hands, and gape as he takes his fingers into his mouth and sucks off all my juices. He flashes me a devilish grin.

Then he leaves me trembling against the wall as he quickly

retrieves a condom from his bag. When he returns to me, he drops his boxers to his ankles and sheathes his cock without preamble.

He looks at me enquiringly, as though asking permission.

Oh God, yes! I nod emphatically and spread my legs.

After a quick check of the condom, he positions himself, pulls my panties aside once more, and enters me. I'm soaking wet, so he slides home with no trouble at all. His balls press tightly against my body as he captures my mouth in a raw, passionate kiss, before pulling away with a feral growl.

He slips his hands around me; lifts one of my legs over his arm to gain better access. Using it as leverage, he thrusts into me like a man possessed. I can do little but loop my arms around his neck and hang on tight. I bite my lip hard to keep from crying out, then taste the coppery twang of blood. The last thing we need is for someone to catch us. Honestly, I'm not too bothered about losing my job—I can always get another one—but there's no way I want this man to stop fucking me until we've both come. And then once more for good measure.

Luciano breathes heavily as he saws in and out of me, a sheen of perspiration across his forehead. His eyes shine as he looks at me. Smiling, he says, "Kayleigh, will you come with me? I cannot stop. You feel so good."

Too breathless to respond, I nod, reach a hand down to my clit and stroke it. This isn't going to take long.

Sure enough, seconds later my pussy tightens deliciously as my orgasm approaches. It grips his thick cock and causes him to bury his head in my shoulder to stifle his moans. As my cunt starts to twitch and spasm, his cock does too. It's fucking divine, and our mouths meet in a hungry, bruising kiss as we are swept up in our respective climaxes. I can't help it—a moan escapes my throat, but I'm too high on lust to care. I cling to him as I come back to earth, until I feel able to move again.

We disentangle silently. Words aren't necessary. Plus, the only one that comes into my head is *wow*. I have no idea if he's ever had sex like that before, but I certainly haven't. My orgasm was mind-blowing—better than anything I've experienced with another man or even with my hands or toys—and luckily for Luciano, it's only served to make me desperate for another one just like it. The man is clearly the master of orgasms. I'm happy to note that the look in his eyes indicates he'd like to give me many more. I bloody hope so.

We dress and tidy ourselves up as best we can, then head out onto the floor for our shift. As we work, our glances are even more furtive and suggestive than they were before. I have no idea if the bosses or any of the other staff have noticed, but if so, nobody's saying anything. Perhaps they don't care—things are so much more laid back in places like this. Who cares if the employees are fucking in the staff room on their break, as long as the customers are being served!

Later, after our shift, he corners me as I grab my things from the staff room. "Kayleigh," he says, glancing out of the open door to make sure we won't be overheard, "are you… okay?"

I frown. Why on earth wouldn't I be okay? He was present for the fuck of my life earlier that evening, and I'm just about to head home as quickly as possible so I can mentally relive it.

It seems he has other ideas.

"I mean, you are okay, with me? You still like me?"

Ah. So he thinks I may regret our staff room misdemeanour. Idiot. Surely the heated looks we've been exchanging all evening ought to have told him that my feelings are quite the opposite. But still, if he needs it spelling out to him…

"Of course I still like you, Luciano. What we did earlier was incredible."

His ego suitably boosted, he beams. "I am glad, it was incredible for me, also. Would you like to do it again?"

There's nothing like a direct question to throw a girl off course. "What, here?"

He laughs. "No, not here. What is the phrase you English use… your place or mine?"

I giggle, surprised at his choice of words. "I don't mind. Wherever is nearest!"

For the second night in a row, I catch a taxi back to my apartment, but this time it's nothing to do with being afraid of walking alone. I simply want to get the sexy Spaniard naked and in my bed as soon as humanly possible. And once he's there, I have no intention of letting him leave until the morning, toilet and shower breaks excepting.

A thrill of anticipation courses through my body. I sense a long night ahead.

We all but burst through the door. Clearly mindful of the fact we're in a private dwelling and don't have to be quiet or worry about someone walking in on us, Luciano slams the door and immediately advances on me. He looks predatory. I fucking love it.

I open my arms and smile as he steps into them, then pull him tightly to me. He captures my lips in a smouldering kiss, and I reach down to grip his luscious arse, moaning into his mouth as I feel the press of his growing erection against me. I want more. So much more. I roll my hips, eager for some friction on my clit.

Obviously sensing my growing need, he pulls away from our kiss and murmurs, "Let's go to the bedroom."

I don't need telling twice. Wordlessly, I take his hand and lead him to my room. Once there, we immediately yank at each other's clothes until we're both naked, then fall onto the bed in a tangle of limbs. It's only when his red-hot cock brushes the bare skin of my thigh that I remember. "Do you have more condoms?"

I send a silent prayer to the gods that his answer will be in the affirmative. I'd been so determined that my only sexual activity on this trip would be with myself and my vibrator, that I hadn't brought any on the trip. I want him, so badly, but I've got no intention of going without protection.

"I do. Do not worry. But we won't need one just yet."

"We won't?"

In lieu of an answer, he shuffles down the bed and parts my thighs, then pushes his head between them. At the first touch of his tongue, I grip the blanket beneath me until my knuckles turn white. God, he's good. His movements are slow yet sure, and in all the right places. Before long, I'm biting my lip again, but this time to avoid scaring the neighbours.

His stubble scratches deliciously against my sensitive inner thighs, and as his tongue teases my clit and makes it grow and tingle, I'm in serious danger of exploding into tiny, bliss-filled pieces. He pulls the fattened nub into his mouth and sucks it gently. I arch my back and claw at the sheets until my hands hurt with the effort.

Lifting his head, he raises an eyebrow at me. "What is the matter, Kayleigh? You do not like it? Should I stop?"

"Stop? Don't you dare!"

I tangle my hands in his thick, dark hair and shove his head back onto my pussy, then groan as he latches onto my clit once more. He grows more passionate, pulling, sucking and occasionally nibbling at it. He's the master of the tease; stopping for a few seconds here and there as though he suspects my orgasm is close. Bastard.

Soon, I can think of little else. He's brought me to the edge so many times I'm worried I'll lose my ability to orgasm altogether; as though my body is punishing me for being with such a tease.

"Luciano," I moan, "please. I need to come. I *want* to come."

He says nothing, merely continues to suckle my swollen clit until my abdomen tightens. I push his face more forcefully into my crotch, rock my hips, desperate to get the extra friction I so desperately need to tip me over the edge.

Just then, he slips two fingers inside my saturated cunt and seeks my G-spot. With a precision that comes only from practice, he manipulates the spongy bundle of flesh until I can't hold back any longer. With a keening cry, I come. My pussy spasms, a gush of hot fluid squirts out around his fingers, and my entire body tumbles into absolute orgasmic bliss.

Losing awareness of my surroundings for a few seconds, I buck and writhe on the bed, wave after wave of pleasure overtaking me. It is heaven.

When I come back to myself, Luciano's rolling a condom down his eager erection. I grin lazily, still a little dopey from my orgasmic out-of-body experience. He returns my smile, then crawls between my legs once more.

"Kayleigh," he strokes his fingers through my cum-soaked pout, "would you like to try something… different?"

"What do you mean?"

He moves his fingers past my perineum and to the tight pucker of muscle below. "Have you ever done it here?" he asks, gently pressing a juicy finger against my anus.

My face fills with heat. "N-no." I shake my head.

He grins, the tip of his finger circling the sensitive flesh. "Would you like to? I promise I will be gentle. Do you have any… lube?"

"Actually," I admit, blushing even harder, "I do."

I may not have any condoms, but I've got a ready supply of batteries for my vibrator, and a bottle of lube. I reach across and open the drawer of my bedside table, retrieve the bottle, and toss it to Luciano.

He hesitates, looking at the lube, then back to me.

"It's okay," I say, lifting my knees towards my chest to give him access to my virgin hole, "I've always wanted to try it. But promise you'll stop if I say."

"Of course," he replies, flicking open the cap and squirting a generous amount of the silky liquid onto his fingertips. "I will make it so good for you."

Hoping he's right, I grab a pillow from the other side of the bed and hold it against my cheek, ready to bite and scream into it if necessary. I pray the only screaming coming from me will be out of pleasure.

Slick sounds ring out as Luciano strokes lube down his latex-covered cock, then more as he squirts more from the bottle.

"It will be cold," he says with a smile.

"Mmm-hmm," I reply, stuffing the pillow into my mouth.

I suck in a hasty breath through my nostrils at the first touch of the cold liquid on my rear hole. However, I quickly forget about the chill as he moves his fingers around and around my anus, before slowly dipping one in. Instinctually, I clench against the intrusion, but Luciano moves his other hand to stroke my buttock, and murmurs, "It is okay, just relax. Push against me, it will make it easier."

Forcing myself to listen to his words, to take them in, I do as he says. Soon he's inside my bottom, up to the knuckle. He slowly pumps his finger in and out of my arse, and I gradually relax as the feeling morphs from strange and alien to incredibly fucking hot.

"That's it," he says, "you are relaxing. Now, would you like me to try two?"

Nodding vigorously, I grunt into the pillow as a second finger stretches me. He again slips inside until I feel the knuckles of his other fingers bumping against my arse.

He continues to prepare me for some minutes, until I'm so unbelievably turned on I tear the pillow away from my face and blurt out, "For fuck's sake, Luciano, just fuck me."

He laughs heartily and removes his fingers. "As you wish."

I hear the snap of the lube bottle lid again, and more chilly liquid is smeared across the entrance to my rear passage. There's a thump as he tosses the bottle onto the floor, then he grasps his cock and positions the head at my slick hole.

"You are sure, Kayleigh? It will hurt a little, but remember to push."

Stuffing the pillow back into my mouth, I grunt my acquiescence. Closing my eyes, I wait for the inevitable pain. As soon as the blunt tip of his prick penetrates me, I push against it. My hole stretches and stretches, and then there's a popping sensation as the head of his cock moves past the tight ring of muscle in my anus. It stings a little, and I suck in a breath, then another as his shaft moves deeper and deeper inside me.

I suddenly remember to breathe, and the pain recedes. It's quickly replaced by pleasure, and my clit swells as my arousal grows, rapidly approaching fever pitch. I gather some of the juices that are pooling in my pussy and slick them over the sensitive bundle of nerve endings.

Luciano watches, rapt, as I move my fingertips in tiny circles around my clit before touching it more directly. The pillow falls from between my teeth as I let out a blissful moan and contract my internal muscles. The motion makes my arse grip tightly around his cock and he grunts, picking up the pace of his thrusts in response.

By now, I'm accustomed to having a cock up my backside and am enjoying it immensely. I push down on his cock, encouraging him to go faster. I need it. Want it. Want him to fuck me hard until I come.

I don't know I've said the words aloud until he replies, "You are making me very horny. If I go much faster, I will come. You are so fucking tight."

"Fuck me, Luciano," I reply breathlessly. "Fuck me hard."

I feel rather like a porn star as I say the words, but I really don't care. I mean them. And boy, does he deliver. He drives into me with a ferocity that makes my eyes roll back in my head, and I rub and pinch at my clit, desperate to wring another orgasm out of my tormented body. My pussy flutters.

Luciano gasps. "Stop that, or I will come."

"I can't help it. I'm close to coming, too."

With that, he digs his fingers into my hips and pumps like a man possessed. I pick up the pace on my clit, sure my hand must be a blur of desperate motion.

Seconds later, I topple over the edge into the most intense orgasm. I'm vaguely aware of Luciano's grunts and moans, and the twitching of his cock deep inside me, but the forefront of my mind is occupied by… utter heaven. Stars burst behind my eyelids as I'm overtaken by pleasure. My internal muscles contract wildly, and a gush of ejaculate bursts from my cunt, covering both me and Luciano where our bodies are joined.

The waves of bliss seem to go on forever, and I surf them willingly. I can hardly believe what I'm experiencing. Luciano has teased reactions from my body I didn't think were possible. I'd heard about them, of course, but had dismissed many of them as fallacy.

I thank my lucky stars. I've clearly bagged myself a very skilled lover, who knows just which buttons to push. And boy, am I pleased he's pushed them. Sighing happily, I feel boneless as I relax into the bed.

Halfway into an almost-doze, I feel Luciano pull out and hear him disappear from the room. The toilet flushes, then there's running water. Soon, he returns and eases me into his arms and against his warm body, murmuring sweet nothings into my ear. Or at least, that's what I think they are. In his post-coital sleepiness, he's lapsed into his native tongue, so I only understand the occasional word here and there. But it doesn't matter; I get the sentiment and curl happily into his embrace as we drift off to sleep.

***

After our spectacular first day—and night—together, I break my man-fast in spectacular style by fucking Luciano at every available opportunity. At work, in our respective apartments, on the beach, in the sea. I have so many orgasms I can barely think straight. We experiment with more anal sex, oral sex, and the usual manner of fucking. It doesn't matter how we do it. We're so horny for each other that one climax is merely a warm up for those that will follow, regardless of how they're achieved.

If things were different, I'd be worried about burning out; about us tiring of each other. But we both know I'm not going to be around forever, so we make the most of our situation while it lasts.

When it's time for me to leave, we part as friends. I'm left with nothing but good memories; and perhaps a few bite marks, scratches and many, many empty condom packets.

I will never, ever forget Luciano. He'll never know, but he seriously raised the bar for my sex life. It will be a long time before I find a man who will compare to him and his amazing sexual prowess. I'll enjoy fantasies about him for many months and years, bringing myself to many blistering orgasms as I do so. The way he looks at me, the way he touches me, the way he fucks me, and the way he makes me come like a bullet train. He's undoubtedly the best part of my gap year.

When I eventually find a man who makes me come like Luciano does, I'll fucking marry him. That way I'm guaranteed a happily ever after.

Trinity's New Hobby

Trinity heard Colton's key in the door, then him calling out. "Hey, Trinity, I'm home!"

"In here," she said, continuing to concentrate on what she was doing, her hands moving methodically, rhythmically.

Footsteps on the wooden floor, then his voice again, closer. "What, not meeting me at the door? Flinging yourself into my arms and welcoming me home, sexy style?"

"I'm not doing anything until I've finished this row," she said without looking up.

Colton tutted. "What *are* you doing, anyway? Crochet? Did an alien steal you away and replace you with a granny who looks exactly like you?" He moved around the sofa and dropped down next to her.

"Hey! Watch it! You nearly made me drop a stitch." Clutching extra hard at her needles, she inspected the work carefully to make sure she hadn't, in fact, dropped a stitch.

Sniggering, Colton shot back, "Sorry, Granny."

She shot him a glare. "It's not funny. I've worked bloody hard on this, and there's no way I want to screw it up now. And in answer to your question, no I'm not crocheting. I'm knitting. I've just started recently. And I haven't been a victim of an alien invasion. I just enjoy it, all right? It's relaxing, and unlike your favourite hobby of watching TV, I actually get something out of this at the end."

Colton shrugged. "Whatever. I like to watch TV to relax, you like to knit." He paused. "You've got to admit it's kinda old-fashioned, though."

Trinity reached the end of her row, carefully put the point-protectors on to stop the garment slipping off the needles, then placed the whole thing down on the coffee table. Turning to her boyfriend with a wry expression, she said, "Actually, I'll have you know, knitting's cool again. Crafting in general is experiencing a massive revival. People are staying in more, wanting to save money. Making gifts instead of buying them..."

"Okay, okay." He held his hands up. "I get it. Knitting's cool." Pointing at the mass of wool on the table, he asked, "What are you making, anyway?"

"A jumper. For myself, before you panic. I'm not going to start making cutesy things with animals or bobbles on and forcing you to wear them."

Colton huffed out a breath. "Thank God for that. Just 'cos you're a granny all of a sudden, doesn't mean I want to start dressing like a granddad."

Fixing her boyfriend with a look that should, by rights, have turned him to stone, Trinity snatched up her knitting and flounced out of the room. She headed for their bedroom, where she kept her knitting stuff neatly in a corner of her wardrobe. As she put her hard work away carefully in her bag, her fingers brushed against a spare length of cut-off yarn. The thick blue wool gave her an idea. Grinning, she gently pulled it out. Yes, it would do nicely.

Just then, she heard Colton muttering to himself, then his progress from the living room to their bedroom. He was probably coming to apologise. She smirked. Well, she'd make him grovel, all right.

Quickly, she grabbed the chair that leaned up against the wall and shifted it into the large space between the bed and the door, with it facing the bed.

Colton walked in just as she'd stepped back, and his gaze alighted on the chair. He frowned, then looked at her. Shaking his head, he adopted a gently-smiling expression. "Look, babe, I'm sorry. I didn't mean to upset you. I was just teasing you, which I know doesn't excuse what I said, but I definitely wasn't trying to hurt you. I don't mind what hobbies you have, as long as you're happy." He paused, his smile growing wider, more hopeful. "Forgive me?"

Giving him a cool smile, she pointed at the chair and snapped, "Sit down."

Frowning again, Colton stepped over to the chair and lowered himself into it. "W-what are you doing?" A look of realisation crossed his face, and his confusion morphed into pure delight. "Ahh, are you gonna give me a lap dance?"

Trinity resisted the temptation to roll her eyes. "Yeah, babe," she said lightly, much more lightly than she felt. "Something like that. Close your eyes."

Clearly convinced it was his lucky day, Colton did as she ordered with a smirk.

Letting her irritation and frustration show on her face now, Trinity crossed over to the chair and stepped behind it. After swiftly pulling the wool out to its full length, she set about securing Colton's wrists to the chair. The yarn was super chunky, but she wasn't sure quite how strong it was, so she wrapped it around twice, making sure it wasn't so tight it would cut off his circulation. Examining her handiwork, Trinity was surprised at herself. They'd never fooled around with bondage before, and yet she'd managed to tie Colton up, quickly and safely. Apparently those smutty books she'd been reading were informative as well as erotic.

"Ooh, getting a little kinky are we, sweetie?" Colton asked. He sounded excited rather than worried, which made Trinity's job easier, not to mention much more fun.

"Yes, darling," she purred, moving to his side, then leaning down and nibbling his earlobe, eliciting a guttural groan from his throat. "I thought a bit of bondage would be fun. So I've tied you up with wool."

"With *wool?*" Colton's eyes flew open, wide open, and he gazed at his girlfriend. "Seriously?" He fidgeted in the seat, wriggling his arms and trying to twist his neck to see the unusual form of bondage.

"Yep. I thought it would be a good idea to show you knitting isn't as boring or as granny-ish as you seem to think."

Colton groaned, this time in disappointment, frustration. "So I'm not getting a lap dance. You're going to sit there, knitting, and make me watch, aren't you?"

Shaking her head, Trinity replied, "No. Though I hadn't thought of that. Any more of your cheek and that's exactly what I'll do. In a way, what I have planned is worse. Much worse."

He opened his mouth to speak, then seemingly thought better of it, and kept quiet.

With a curt nod, Trinity flashed Colton what she hoped was a seductive grin and began to undress. He remained silent, transfixed as she tugged off her jumper, then the T-shirt beneath. Bending slowly, giving Colton a tantalising view of her breasts hanging heavily in her bra, she removed her socks, then kicked the pile of shed clothes away from her. Next, she spun around, undoing her belt, then the button and zip of her jeans. She unhurriedly inched them down, now treating him to the vision of her exposed buttocks, bisected by her lacy black thong, and her thighs, too, as the jeans bunched up around her ankles.

Before long, she stepped out of them, shoving them towards the other items she'd removed. Now, with equal speed—or lack of it—she slipped down her panties. Once they were on the pile, leaving her utterly naked, she flashed Colton her wickedest grin, biting her bottom lip.

He strained at his bonds, but it was fruitless—the super chunky yarn was doing a good job, albeit not the one it had been intended for.

Satisfied Colton wasn't going anywhere, Trinity settled back on the bed, still facing him. She was going to give him a show and a half. First, she sucked the index and middle fingers of her right hand into her mouth, getting them good and wet. Slicking the saliva over each of her nipples in turn, she repeated the process, then began to tweak the rapidly hardening buds.

It wasn't long before she felt slickness between her thighs. Because her plan had formed and been carried out so fast, there'd been no anticipation, no time for her body to catch on. But ever since she'd tied Colton up and begun stripping in front of him, her libido had gradually ramped up. Now, as she plucked at her tits, zings of delicious arousal licked their way along her nerve endings, pooling in her groin. Already her labia were growing fat, and her clit throbbed.

Forcing herself to hold on longer, just a little bit longer, to draw out Colton's agony, she grew rougher with her nipples. Her rolls and squeezes became full-on tugs and pinches, elongating the sensitive flesh and drawing moans and groans from her parted lips.

A glance at Colton told Trinity that she was most definitely having the desired effect, and she hadn't even touched her pussy yet, or even shown it to him. She decided it was time for both of those things. Leaning back on her left hand, she parted her legs and slipped her right hand between them.

Colton made a strangled sound as her sex was revealed to him, already wet and swollen, and so close but ultimately out of reach. Trinity played around, dipping her fingers just inside her cunt and swiping the juices over her vulva and clit. Again and again she touched and teased, until she couldn't hold back any longer. Her boyfriend's expression, his blatant need for her was as arousing as her touch, and now her clit ached so much it was almost painful.

Scooping up more of the copious fluid that flowed from her, Trinity stroked it over her clit, jolting slightly at the sensitivity she found there. It wouldn't take much to make her come, that much was obvious. Zoning in on the tiny spot near the bundle of nerve endings that really got her going, she rubbed, building up to exactly the pressure and rhythm she needed. At the same time, she watched

Colton watching her, and got a huge kick from how he reacted to her every move; his eyes wide, jaw slack, his fidgeting and the probably-unconscious jerking of his hips.

Splaying her thighs even wider to ensure Colton was getting a really good view, she continued masturbating without holding back, every movement bringing her closer to climax. It wouldn't be long...

Throwing her head back, she picked up her pace, not caring about the discomfort in her right hand. Coming was more important in that instant, and, as the tightening in her abdomen increased, the tingles between her legs began, she knew she was on the precipice.

Apparently Colton knew, too. "God, oh God, babe, you look so fucking hot. Please let me fuck you."

Ignoring him, Trinity let her fingers push her over the edge, an almighty climax crashing into her, making her cunt clench, her juices flow and her throat hoarse with her cries. It took all of the energy she had to stay relatively upright, as she wanted to watch her boyfriend's reaction as she came right there in front of him, not allowing him to do anything except watch.

Her pleasure held her in its grip of oblivion for several long seconds, but as soon as she broke free enough, she opened her eyes again and looked at him.

Mouth agape, eyes almost popping out of his head, and with an erection threatening to burst from his trousers, it seemed he'd definitely enjoyed the show.

"So," she said, snapping her legs shut and fixing him with a stern look, "still think I'm a granny?"

Colton shook his head so fast he probably gave himself neck strain. He looked so eager, so damn horny, that she almost took pity on him.

Almost.

Farm Hand

As Ramona made her way down the gravel track, she spotted some farm buildings. She glanced down at her map, then nodded. Her route would take her right through the farmyard and over a stile into the adjacent field.

She just hoped she didn't meet any hostile dogs. Or geese. She shuddered. Geese could be vicious creatures.

As she grew closer to the yard, Ramona saw someone hefting bales of hay off a truck. She let out a sigh of relief. At least the farmer would be able to control any unruly animals.

When he turned to place a hay bale on the ground, Ramona saw the man in profile. He was younger than she'd expected. Much younger. As his powerful body moved beneath his clothes, Ramona watched, open-mouthed. All thoughts of scary dogs and geese had been erased from her mind. She was still drawing closer to him, though her steps were stealthier now. She didn't want him to know she was there just yet—she was enjoying the flex of his muscles far too much to want to disturb him.

She was now close enough to make out his features. *Mmm, not your typical farmer. This guy is hotter than the surface of the sun.*

Ramona stopped at the end of the lane, still within the cover of the trees and hedges lining it. The farmer continued working, heaving the hay around as though it were feathers. It didn't look as though anyone else was around. He unloaded the lorry without pausing. The only sign of his exertion was the brief sweep of his sleeve across his forehead, mopping up the sweat that threatened to trickle down his face.

Ramona was in danger of some trickling of her own, only
much lower down. Then, just as she thought she'd better stop ogling
and get on with her walk, he stopped. She froze. Had he seen her
lurking in the shadowy lane? He didn't turn, didn't call out. Perhaps
it was the beating sun and his workload getting to him.

After a moment, he grabbed the hem of his shirt and tugged
the garment up and over his head. Then he carelessly balled it up and
tossed it into the cab of the truck. Ramona suppressed a lusty moan
as she drank in his front view. Hotter than the surface of the sun had
been a completely apt description.

The farmer's long, lean body tapered down into narrow hips,
from which hung loose combat trousers. They were slung so low she
could see the line of dark hair running from his bellybutton
southwards.

Completely oblivious to his appreciative audience, the farmer
started moving the bales into a nearby barn. Ramona enjoyed every
detail as he did so; the dusting of dark hair on his broad chest, his
muscular arms, handsome face and *ohhh*—she bit her lip as he bent
over—his tight backside.

Any minute now, his wife was going to come out with a cool
drink—Ramona was sure of it. There was no way a man this
attractive hadn't been snapped up. She waited. Nobody came.

By now, Ramona was getting really rather agitated. The
gusset of her knickers was wet. It stuck to her skin, and her pussy
ached. She stuffed her hand between her thighs and squeezed them
together, hoping the friction would provide some relief. It didn't. If

anything, it just made things worse.

Across the yard, the hard-working hunk wiped his brow again, then glanced at his watch. A surprised expression crossed his attractive features. Ramona checked her own watch. Lunchtime.

There were only a few stacks of hay left to be taken into the barn. It was obvious what was going to happen. He was going to put the last few bales away and head indoors for lunch, leaving Ramona there, insanely horny and unable to do anything about it. She wasn't even halfway through her walk, so wasn't as if she could rush home to stroke herself to climax.

Her brain whirred, flicking through a multitude of devious plans, none of which seemed plausible.

The sweaty sex god walked out of the barn once more, having deposited his last load, and moved in the direction of the farmhouse.

Ramona's hormones took over and forced her brain into a quick—and probably quite reckless—decision. Before she knew what she was doing, she'd stepped out of the lane, pretended to turn her ankle, and gone down with a loud yelp, her map slapping the rough concrete next to her.

Within seconds, the farmer ran over, muscles flexing and sunlight glinting on his sweat-damp skin.

Ramona swallowed the saliva pooling in her mouth. She was going for damsel in distress, not drooling mess.

"Hey, are you okay?" Stupid question aside, the farmer's deep, seductive voice made Ramona hotter still. God, she wanted him. If he turned her down, then fine. She'd just have to go home and wank herself silly. But she was going to give it her best shot.

He crouched beside her, already reaching for her "injured" ankle. He wore no wedding ring. Adrenaline pumped through Ramona's body and her heart fluttered. She mentally shook herself—that didn't mean a thing. He probably didn't wear it for work in case he lost or damaged it. Or perhaps he had a girlfriend, but wasn't married yet.

When he touched her, Ramona's brain promptly disengaged from that thought process.

"Ooh," she moaned, then remembered to sound uncomfortable, rather than aroused, "ouch. I turned it on a stone or something."

Long, skilful fingers gently pressed and prodded. Even through her thick walking socks, the power in his hands was apparent. Dirty thoughts filled her head. Thoughts about what else he could do with those hands. And fingers. And tongue. And cock.

"Do you think you can walk?" he asked.

Ramona glanced doubtfully at her ankle, lips twisting in a wry grin.

Grabbing the discarded map and passing it to her, he said, "Take off your backpack and hold it. I'll carry you."

At this point, she'd have run naked around the yard if he'd asked her to. She slipped her arms from the thick straps, stuffed the map into a pocket, then clutched the pack to her chest.

"Okay?" he asked. "Ready?"

She nodded. A moment later he lifted her like she was a bag of sugar. Or one of his haybales. She was pressed against his firm body, which was still slick with sweat. As she wrapped an arm around the back of his neck to steady herself, she decided she thoroughly enjoyed being a damsel in distress. Of course it helped that her rescuer was totally gorgeous.

The farmer's thick, dark hair curled into his neck, just millimetres from her fingertips. She barely resisted the temptation to plunge her digits into the strands and pull his lips to hers.

Ramona frowned as he began walking towards the barn.

Catching her expression, he said, "It's closer than the house. Plus there are no closed doors to contend with. I'd just like to get you into the shade and look at your ankle properly."

And I'd just like to get you naked and look at your cock properly. Biting her lip to prevent a smirk, she blinked as they were suddenly swallowed into the shade of the barn.

Her knight in shining armour, clearly familiar with the layout of the building, didn't break stride. He propelled them deeper into the relative gloom, then made a beeline for—perhaps unsurprisingly—a stack of hay.

Bending carefully to grab a sheet from a nearby workbench, he gingerly gripped it in his fingertips, careful not to drop Ramona. Then, moving to the bales, he said, "Can you stand on your good leg for a few seconds while I put this down? Hold on to me if you need to."

He lowered Ramona gently to the ground. She frantically tried to remember which ankle was "affected" so as to put the correct leg down. As her weight rested on the leg, she put her hands on his waist to steady herself as he spread the sheet over the hay.

Ramona was disappointed when he said, "Okay, you can sit down." She'd been rather enjoying the hard, damp planes of muscle beneath her fingers.

She sat, wondering what he'd do next. Ramona certainly hadn't been prepared for him to walk back across the barn, stick his head out of the yawning expanse of door frame, look from side to side, then drag the door closed.

Her heart raced. What the fuck was going on? She started to panic. Had she been inadvertently lusting over a psychopath? Was he going to chop her into pieces and feed her to the pigs?

Before her imagination could wander any further, he was back at her side.

"Wh-what did you do that for?" she asked.

"My mum's in the house. I didn't want to risk her coming out and disturbing us. She'll never move that door without us hearing it."

She frowned. "Y-your mum?"

"Yes. My dad's at market today, which is why I'm on my own."

"Oh."

"So, where were we?"

"You were going to look at my ankle. I think it might be sprained."

"There's nothing wrong with your ankle and we both know it."

"Wha—there is!"

"So how come you changed ankles from the yard to the barn?

Injury run up one leg and down the other, did it?"

Bollocks. His sweaty sexiness had obviously turned her brain to mush. She said nothing.

"Plus I saw you watching me from the lane. Your bright red T-shirt didn't exactly help you blend in with the surroundings."

She looked down. It was true. Her T-shirt wasn't exactly a muted colour. Ramona suspected her face was now a similar shade of scarlet.

"So," he said, "why were you watching me? Are you some kind of pervert?"

Wetness pooled in her pussy at his stern tone. It gave Ramona a hunch, and she decided to act on it. "And what if I am?" she said, quirking an eyebrow at him.

"Well then. Perhaps we'd better give your filthy mind something to think about."

He reached down, hooked his fingers under the edge of the offending T-shirt, and slid it up Ramona's body, over her head and dropped it to the floor. Her black lacy bra was revealed in all its glory.

"That's a very sexy bra, young lady. Especially for going hiking. Now, I can't help but wonder if your panties match."

He knelt and deftly unlaced her heavy boots before removing them. Then he took off her socks. Finally, he straightened. Even on his knees, his height put him in a perfectly kissable position. He obviously thought so too.

He slipped a hand behind Ramona's head and pulled her to him. As their lips crushed together, she sucked in a hasty breath through her nostrils. Big mistake. The scent of the farmer's fresh sweat and a faint twinge of cologne was heady.

As he plunged his tongue between her lips, Ramona's senses went into overdrive. Not only did he look, sound, feel and smell delicious; he tasted it too. He'd obviously been chewing gum or eating mints as the tongue sliding sensuously against her own was pleasantly minty. She moaned into his mouth.

He pulled back with a smirk. "Horny?"

"What do you think?"

"I think I'd like to find out for sure. And then there's the mystery of the matching underwear."

His hands went to her waist and made short work of the button and zip of her hiking trousers. Then he pushed her gently onto her back and pulled them down.

"Hmm," he said, inspecting her plain black thong. "It doesn't quite match. Never mind, it's coming off anyway."

Good to his word, he grabbed the sides of the thong and tugged it down. As the sticky gusset unpeeled from her skin, Ramona cringed, hoping he wouldn't notice just how sodden it was. No such luck. Her cream was clearly visible on the black cotton.

He laughed. "Just what were you doing behind that hedge, you dirty bitch?"

Without giving her a chance to answer, he tossed the thong to the floor. Then he slipped his hands beneath her legs and pulled her to the very edge of the hay bale. After parting her thighs, he let out a grunt of satisfaction and began to lick her pussy.

He made a pleased-sounding noise as her juices flooded his

mouth. Ramona arched her back as the sound vibrated against her sensitive flesh. He took this as encouragement and redoubled his efforts, increasing the pressure. He swirled his tongue across her skin, inching closer to her clitoris, but maddeningly moving away again. She was sure he was doing it on purpose. *Bastard.* She reached forward and tangled her fingers in his thick hair. It was just long enough to hold on to, and she tugged him into position until his lips finally met her clit.

Sweet Jesus. She was so aroused that the slightest touch was torture. A squeal escaped her as he sucked the sensitive bundle of nerve endings into his mouth. He continued to pull and nibble at her tormented flesh until a shiver wracked her body. His eyes met hers. He moved back, allowing her clit to pop from his mouth.

"You gonna come for me, baby?"

She nodded frantically. "For God's sake, don't stop until I do."

"Oh, don't worry. I won't. Not until your cum is dribbling down my chin."

Ramona didn't think it was possible to be any hornier, but his filthy words pushed her higher. Her cunt contracted involuntarily and suddenly she really wanted to feel his cock inside her. Filling her, stretching her, pounding her until she screamed. "Please, just hurry up and fuck me."

"All in good time. I want your juices dribbling down my face first."

With that, he buried his face back in her wetness. He ate her pussy with gusto, licking up every drop of her cream, then closing his lips around her clit again. This time, he didn't stop or pull away. He sucked that tingling button of flesh until Ramona's orgasm hit with force, causing her to buck and twist beneath him. White spots danced before her eyes and a strangled noise spilled out of her mouth, followed by a multitude of expletives. Still he kept his head between her legs, lapping at her until finally she lay still.

Only then did he sit up, grinning widely. And the grin wasn't the only thing on his face. A sheen coated the area around his mouth. He licked his lips. "Fuck me, you taste good. I can't wait to get inside you." Then he paused, his face dropping. "Shit. I don't suppose you have a condom?"

Ramona almost considered shaking her head, rather than facing the shame of admitting she had condoms in her backpack. But she wanted him inside her, so she nodded sheepishly. Pointing languidly at her bag, she said, "My purse is in the inside pocket. There's one in there."

He was obviously as desperate to fuck as she, as he grabbed the bag without hesitation and quickly sought the elusive purse. Seconds later, he made a triumphant noise and turned back to her, foil packet in hand. He tore it open carefully before stuffing the wrapper into his pocket.

Looking down at his heavy-duty lace-up boots, he murmured, "Fuck that, I'll leave 'em on."

After moving back over to where Ramona lay, he used one hand to undo his combats, then shoved them and his boxers down in one go, letting them fall to his ankles. Then he encouraged Ramona to make room for him on the hay. As she backed up, he crawled quickly after her. Once they were both safely positioned, he knelt between her legs. He maintained heated eye contact with her as he rolled the condom on, so she only got a brief glimpse of his cock before he leaned down to kiss her. But that glimpse had been enough to know she wouldn't be disappointed.

As his tongue slipped into her mouth, his shaft nudged up against her vulva. She lifted her hips, desperate for him to fill her. He remained resolutely still for a little longer, kissing her with a fervour that let on just how much he wanted her. Then, without warning, he dipped his hips, pressed his cock between her pussy lips, and continued to push until he was balls-deep inside her. It was a move that left Ramona gasping. She squeezed her internal muscles, causing him to moan into her mouth.

He broke their kiss, then lifted himself up and looked down at where their bodies were joined, then back at her face. "You are so fucking tight. If I go too fast, I won't be able to hold back for long."

"Go for it. Give me everything you've got."

As the words left her mouth, Ramona wondered what on earth she was letting herself in for. With his fitness level, she may well have to bite her lip to avoid his mother running in from the house to see who was being murdered.

As he began to thrust in and out of her, she stopped thinking about anything but how she was feeling. How he felt inside her, his cock pressed tightly up against her G-spot and his pubic bone grinding against her clit. Fuck, this guy knew what he was doing. She grasped his buttocks and enjoyed the sensation of them beneath her hands, the hard muscles flexing beneath rounded flesh. As he picked up his pace, she dug her nails into his arse cheeks, causing him to grunt and fuck her harder still. It was a vicious circle, albeit a pleasurable one.

Before long, Ramona felt the delicious build up between her thighs that signalled the onset of her orgasm. And, it appeared, not a moment too soon.

"I'm not gonna be able to hold on much longer," her lover said, gritting his teeth. "You just feel so damn good."

"I'm almost there," she whispered breathlessly. "Just fuck me. Please."

And he did. He fucked her so furiously that she felt like her pussy was on fire. Pulling and clutching at his arse, she murmured words and phrases of encouragement until her approaching orgasm rendered her silent.

She arched her back, urging him deeper and deeper. Then she toppled over the edge. Her climax ripped ferociously through her body and her cunt gripped his cock and milked it for all it was worth. Their cries echoed through the barn and Ramona dug her nails so hard into his fleshy buttocks that later, she wondered if she'd broken the skin. But there and then, swept away on her own wave of bliss, she didn't care.

As they came down from their glorious highs, he rolled over next to her and they lay in a companionable silence as their breathing and heart rates slowed.

After a while, the companionable silence became awkward, and Ramona decided to make her move. She'd got what she wanted, after all. She sat up, then climbed off the bales and began to locate her scattered clothing.

"You're leaving?"

Ramona turned. Her pussy gave a lurch at the sight of her lover, looking dishevelled and quite literally fucked. "Yes. I have to finish my walk before it gets dark."

"Okay." He didn't press the matter, despite the fact there were plenty of hours of daylight remaining.

They dressed in silence and then he rolled open the heavy barn door to let her out, blinking, into the sunlight. She shouldered her backpack and, unsure what to do, she gave him a wry smile and said, "See you around."

Then she turned and headed, on still-trembling legs, for the stile she'd been aiming for what felt like hours ago. Just as she stepped over it, she heard a noise behind her. She paused with one leg either side of the stile and looked to see him approaching. When he arrived at the stile, he reached for her hand and pressed a crumpled piece of paper into it.

"My number," he said with a smile. "So you can let me know the next time you'll be walking through my farmyard."

She blushed, surprised that he seemed to want to see her again. "Thanks—"

Her eyes widened as she realised that not only had she fucked a random stranger on a whim, but she didn't even know his name. Or he hers.

"John," he supplied, sensing her embarrassment.

"Thanks, John. I'm Ramona."

With that, she zipped his number safely into her trouser

pocket and went on her way, leaving the hunky farmer gazing bemusedly after her for a few minutes before he turned and headed inside for his lunch. After all, he'd well and truly earned it.

What's All This Then?

Madison was bored. She still had a couple of hours left of her shift and it was dragging. There was absolutely nothing going on; no break-ins, muggings, domestic violence, or even anyone being drunk and disorderly. It was unheard of for a Saturday night. She almost wished that someone would commit a crime, just so she had something to do.

She decided to drive out of town. There was a road on the outskirts that was quiet in the evening. Youngsters tended to congregate there, drinking, smoking weed, and generally misbehaving. Perhaps she'd be able to bust a couple of kids for possession or something. She could but hope.

Madison drove the squad car through town and out towards her destination. Leaving the street lights of civilisation behind, she flicked on headlights' main beam. As she travelled further down the road she expected to hear the revving of engines. Silly racer boys with their souped-up cars and equally silly girls hanging off their arms often hung around here. But no, the only sound was that of Madison's car engine and the tyres on the tarmac.

God, is this shift ever *going to end?* She planned to motor to the end of the road and head back to the station via another route. However, before she got much further, she saw a car parked in a layby. She mentally rejoiced; this was bound to be someone up to no good. If it wasn't smoking drugs or drinking, then at the very least it'd be a couple of spotty teenagers canoodling. If so, she could put a flea in their ear and send them packing.

Pulling in behind the car, she killed her lights. If they hadn't noticed her already, they were clearly otherwise occupied. Madison didn't want to alert them to her presence and give them chance to stop what they were doing before she could catch them in the act.

She got out of the car, pulled on her hat, and checked everything she needed was attached to her belt. She doubted there'd be any trouble, but it was always better to be prepared. Silencing her radio, Madison approached the car; the last thing she needed was it suddenly crackling into life just as she was about to witness someone using illegal substances.

It was a clear night and the moon shone down brightly, illuminating the scene. Madison studied the car, surprised. It wasn't your typical boy-racer-mobile. In fact, it was a very expensive car. Perhaps the driver had borrowed Daddy's car. Either that or it was stolen. *Bingo*.

It wasn't until Madison drew level with the boot of the car that she realised there was quite a lot of movement coming from the car. In an up-and-down fashion. The penny dropped. It was looking more likely that Madison was going to be making mention of the words "indecent exposure" as opposed to "illegal substances." Either way, the evening had suddenly become much more interesting.

Madison stepped up to look through the car's rear window. Even in the gloom, it was clear what was going on. These two had gone way beyond the indecent exposure stage. They were full on "at it." The couple's heads were on the opposite side of the car, so she couldn't glimpse their faces. All she could see were bobbing bum cheeks and splayed legs. However, it was obvious that these were no spotty teenagers. These were adults, and the car obviously belonged to them. Or one of them, at least.

As she raised her hand to rap on the window, something stopped her. She continued to watch the rutting couple through the window. Madison had never had herself down as a voyeur, but something about this situation was affecting her. The man's tight buttocks were bouncing up and down, gripped and squeezed in the hands of the woman he was fucking. He had a broad back and muscular arms and legs. From this angle at least, he was definitely eye candy. The way they were going, she couldn't work out how the windows weren't steaming up. Then she spotted all four windows were open a crack. They'd obviously done this before.

She moved closer. She could see more detail now. One of the woman's legs was around her lover's back, the other hooked over the driver's seat. This was one flexible lady. Madison's position meant that when the guy pulled back, she could see his meaty cock parting the swollen pussy lips of his partner, before thrusting back inside her.

Her own pussy fluttered. The thought of being fucked senseless by that cock, any cock in fact, was getting her juices flowing. So were the noises emanating from within the vehicle. Ecstatic grunts and moans spilled forth and Madison's senses went into overdrive. She imagined herself as the woman; being pounded in the back of a car where anybody could catch them. The heat between her legs increased, and juices started to seep into her underwear.

Madison was startled from her reverie as the movement in the car stopped. She froze, thinking they'd seen her standing there and that all hell was about to break loose. Fortunately, they hadn't. They were simply changing position. Nevertheless, Madison ducked away from the window. The guy's sheer size and bulk had prevented the woman from being able to see over his shoulder before, but she wasn't about to take any risks.

After some less rhythmic jigging from the car, Madison heard a giggle, followed by the much deeper rumble of the man's laugh. Creeping back to the window and peering in, she saw they were now in the doggy-style position. Luckily, facing away from her. With two rear views almost in her face, Madison could see everything there was to see. The woman's cunt was wide open and slick with juices. The man was rubbing his cock up and down her seam, coating his shaft with her wetness.

Madison's own pussy was getting very wet and her clit ached for attention. She wanted to be teased the way the man was teasing his lover, slipping his prick in between her folds and out again, without actually penetrating her. He was exercising impressive restraint by not plunging back inside and continuing to fuck the woman's brains out.

Seconds later, she found out why. He had an ulterior motive. After slipping a hand between their bodies, the guy pushed his fingers inside his lover's slippery hole, then removed them. He smeared the natural lubrication over her arsehole, before repeating the process. Then he positioned his cock head at her rear entrance and slowly penetrated her.

Madison's eyes widened. He was fucking her up the arse! And, judging from the noises she was making, she loved it. She watched, fascinated, as the woman's tight hole gobbled up her man's cock. Soon, he was buried inside her to the hilt, his balls crushed between their bodies. Pausing momentarily, presumably to let his lover's body get used to the invasion, the man then began to move with shallow thrusts in and out of her grasping hole.

Madison couldn't take it anymore. The live sex show playing out in front of her was making her unbelievably horny. She was going to have to do something about it. Her pussy burned with need, her clit throbbing. She unzipped her fly and slipped a hand inside, glad the design of her uniform trousers gave her plenty of room to do so. She slid her fingers beneath the waistband of her knickers, then reached down and touched herself. Unsurprisingly, she was saturated.

Dipping her fingers between her pussy lips, Madison found her clit swollen and sensitive to the touch. She slicked her juices over the aching bud, then started to stroke in tiny circles, all the while watching the action taking place inside the car. The guy was now fucking the woman's arse as roughly as he'd fucked her cunt. Surely, if they carried on like that, he was going to come any moment?

Would he come inside her bum? Or would he pull out and spunk on her arse and back? Madison had never been taken that way herself and tried to imagine what it would feel like; both having a cock up there and to have a man ejaculate inside her bottom. It obviously didn't hurt if done right; the woman's cries were of pleasure, not pain. Madison rubbed harder at her clit now, fingers sliding effortlessly over juice-slicked flesh.

One of the man's hands had now snaked between his lover's legs. The motion of his arm indicated that he was stroking her clit, just as Madison was stroking her own. God, she really wished she was the one in the car, being stroked and fucked.

An intense, sublime tingling began in Madison's abdomen. She quickly snatched her hand away. Although she desperately wanted to come, her climax was likely to be so powerful she'd find it difficult not to make a noise. She couldn't risk them hearing or seeing her. The potential repercussions were unthinkable.

Meanwhile, it seemed the couple were heading towards their own grand finale. The man's arm pumped up and down as he busily frotted away at the woman's clit, and his cock plundered her arse. Their grunts and cries were growing steadily louder. Unable to resist, Madison put her fingertips back on her clit and worked it slowly. If she kept herself teetering on the edge long enough, she figured a few well-timed strokes would make her come just as they did, and then their cries could drown out her own.

She didn't have to figure for long. Just as Madison reached the stage of having to grit her teeth to try to keep control, the woman reached her peak. A moment's quiet ensued, before her keening cry resulted in lots more frantic thrusting from her lover.

Madison's time was now. Ending the agony on her tortured clit, she gave a series of swift, firm rubs and felt the blissful waves start to take over her body. Simultaneously, the man shouted out a string of expletives and an almost animal grunt as he reached his own peak.

Fortunately, Madison's stifled cry, released into her sleeve, was lost. She dug her teeth into the stiff material of her jacket as the force of her climax almost brought her to her knees. Her soaking pussy grasped and twitched at nothing, and a delicious heat snaked through her. She rode out the climax, her legs shaking uncontrollably, barely holding her up.

Moments later, when she was capable of rational thought and movement once more, Madison shook herself. She really ought to figure out what she was going to do next. If the pair fell asleep, she was home free. She could get back in the car and be gone, and nobody would be any the wiser. If not, maybe she'd have to pretend she'd only just arrived and give them a bollocking. They wouldn't know the difference; the amount of noise they'd been making would have easily drowned out the sound of her approach.

Looking up, Madison's heart almost stopped. The couple were peering out of the window, straight at her. Under normal circumstances, this would have been a good time to act out the plan she'd just concocted in head. Trouble was, she still had her hand inside her trousers. Not even the best liar in the world would be able to come up with a believable excuse for that.

Heart pounding, Madison snatched her hand out, then hurriedly did up her fly. What the fuck was she going to do now? Before her brain could come up with something, however, the car door opened. The man, clad only in his jeans, stepped out. His lover stayed in the car, still naked and grinning wildly.

"Well, well, well," he said, looking down at her, a sardonic smirk on his face, "what's all this then?"

Loose Ends

When Kat had called to tell me about the five-year university reunion, my reaction had been, "So?"

"Whaddya mean, *so*? You have to come! It'll be a laugh. We'll be able to find out how everyone's getting on, what they've done with their lives and stuff."

"Why do you want to know how everyone's getting on? You've never bothered before, and nor have I. I've only ever kept in touch with you and Alex, and there's a bloody good reason for that. Plus, there's always Facebook if you want to be nosey."

"Come on, not everyone was that bad. There might be some interesting stories to hear. Somebody could be rich, or famous. Or both!"

I stopped resisting. When Kat had a plan, objection was futile.

So there I was, with Kat and Alex, heading into the student union bar. I pushed open the double doors and we entered. It was like we'd walked into some kind of time warp. The bar itself looked almost the same, a lick of paint here and there, but nothing major. As for the people, they seemed to have changed even less. Sure, they were better dressed—well, some of them were—and a little older, but everyone was the same.

The loner was still loitering at the very end of the bar, not engaging with anyone. The geeks had gravitated towards one another. The popular kids were strutting their stuff, their conversation no doubt as mindless and dull as it had always been. Kat, Alex and I were still hanging around together.

Nobody seemed to have brought partners. I hadn't actually seen any information regarding the event. My intel had all come from Kat, so maybe partners weren't invited. Or, perhaps, everyone just wanted to come alone and re-enact their young, free and single days.

Either way, it was going to be a looong night. I made for the bar, with Kat and Alex close behind.

"What'll it be?" said the barman, clearly a current student earning some extra cash. I suddenly felt old, despite there only being around half a decade between us.

"Make mine a vodka and Coke, no ice, please."

As I turned to the girls to find out what they wanted, I saw the class busybody walking towards us. She smiled and waved at me.

"Better make that a double," I amended. Then, under my breath, "I think I'm gonna need it."

Less than a minute later, I remembered why I hadn't been up for this reunion in the first place. The busybody was driving me up the wall. My face and neck were starting to hurt from all the smiling and nodding. Jenny was currently on maternity leave from her *wonderful* job. Her *perfect* husband had stayed home to look after their *delightful* children so she could come to the reunion and see how everyone was getting on. Despite this statement, she hadn't asked any of us a single question. She was too busy talking about herself.

I zoned out of Jenny's inane chatter and stared into space. Suddenly, something moved into my eyeline that snapped me back into the land of the living. Or should I say some*one.*

"Fuck!" I exclaimed, earning myself a disapproving look from Jenny, and puzzled ones from the girls. "He's fucking here!"

Jenny, subtle as ever, started spinning her head around to see who I was talking about, all the while grumbling about "unnecessary bad language". She'd always been a stuck-up bitch.

Kat and Alex, though, knew exactly who I was talking about. Huddling close to me, they started barraging me with questions:

"Whereabouts?"

"How does he look?"

"Is he still hot?"

"Has he seen you?"

"Are you going to talk to him?"

I held up a hand, silencing them. Then I brought the other hand, which was clutching my glass of vodka and Coke, up to my mouth. I finished the contents in a couple of gulps. Following a pause to let the alcohol go down and hopefully settle my nerves, I replied, "What is he even *doing* here? Last I heard, he was working abroad. Dubai or something."

"Well," said Kat, ever the practical one, "why don't you go and ask him?" She gave me a little shove.

"I will," I said decisively, resulting in surprised looks from both girls. "After I've been to the toilet."

Before they could contradict me, I dashed off, leaving my empty glass on the bar. Once in the safety of a locked cubicle, I dropped the toilet seat and sat, head in my hands. I had *not* been prepared for this. Not one bit.

The guy in question had been in most of my classes during my three years at university. He was also "the one who got away." The "one" so many of us have, still loitering in the back of our minds years after the event. In this case, though, his sudden appearance had thrust him so violently to the very front of my mind I was surprised the inside of my cranium didn't hurt.

I'd fancied him almost as soon as I set eyes on him, during our very first day at uni. With his shaggy hair, more-lazy-than-designer stubble and cheeky blue eyes, he was most definitely on my radar.

By happy coincidence, I ended up next to him in the line for induction as we queued to sort out our student IDs, library cards, fee payments and the like. As I stepped up behind him, I checked out his rear view. And boy, was it a view. This guy *knew* how to wear a pair of jeans. He rose even further in my estimation.

I stood there, trying to think of a cool and interesting way to get his attention and introduce myself when that luxury was taken away from me. A group of people pushed past the line, and one of them accidentally caught the edge of my bag, propelling it forward so it fell off my shoulder and smacked him in the back of the leg.

He spun round just as I bent to retrieve my bag, meaning that as I started to straighten up I came face to face with his crotch. My face grew so hot you could have fried bacon on it. I stood abruptly, wishing the ground would swallow me up. "I'm so sorry," I blurted. "Those people walked past and one of them knocked my bag off my shoulder."

"Don't worry about it," he said with a shrug. "It was an

accident. Are you okay?"

I nodded, aware I probably still resembled a tomato.

Sensing my obvious discomfort, he said, "Honestly, it's fine. I'm Jonathan, by the way."

He smiled then, revealing dimples in both cheeks, little crinkles around his eyes, and not-quite-perfect teeth. In that moment, he went from being on my radar to wiping everyone else off it. I was smitten.

I smiled back, then realised he was expecting me to speak. I struggled to get my brain to engage with my mouth. For some reason, all my blood appeared to have rushed elsewhere. "Hi Jonathan. I'm Lauren."

"Nice to meet you. Though you could have just said hello in the first place, rather than throwing things at me, you know."

I opened my mouth to give an indignant retort, then spotted his suppressed smirk. He was teasing me!

And that was how it started. We spent the entire day doing dull admin stuff together and getting to know each other. It should have been the start of a beautiful relationship, but sadly, it wasn't. Because, unfortunately, Jonathan had a girlfriend. We continued to be good friends—albeit with lots of hot and heavy flirting and one hell of a spark—but by the time his relationship came to a natural close, I had a boyfriend. And so a vicious circle continued for three long years, dotted with lots of horniness, longing looks and double entendres; until graduation put an end to the whole sorry state of affairs.

We'd kept in touch sporadically, which was how I knew

we'd still never been single at the same time. I'd think about him during my bouts of singledom, wondering what could have been and imagining the hot sex we'd definitely have had. Given the chance, we'd have been perfect for each other. But by the time I heard he was going to work abroad, Jonathan was nothing but occasional fantasy fodder.

So my surprise when I saw him in the student union bar was amplified by the tumult of feelings that suddenly washed over me. Shock, regret, delight, and the one reaction he'd always managed to get from me—arousal. As I hadn't been prepared for any of those emotions, I needed some time out.

Hence my hiding in the toilets, head in my hands. After a few minutes of wondering what to do, I mentally kicked myself. What on earth was I getting so worked up about? Nothing had ever happened between us; we'd never fallen out, or stopped being friends. We'd simply drifted apart. So there was absolutely no reason in the world I shouldn't just go over and say hi. That was what any normal person would do.

I resolved to be normal, for a change. I lifted the lid and used the toilet while I was there, then came out and washed my hands, splashed some water on my face and touched up my lipstick. A quick spritz of perfume and I was ready to face the world.

When I emerged, I caught sight of Kat and Alex, who had managed to get rid of Jenny. They were keeping themselves entertained by chatting up the barman, by the looks of it. I went over to them. I figured I may as well get a drink, since they already had the barman's attention.

"Oh, hey," Kat said as I reached them. "You're back. Have you been to speak to him already? What happened?"

"No, I've only just come back from the loo. I was coming to get another drink."

"Don't be so ridiculous!" hissed Alex, surprising me and Kat. She was usually the mild-mannered one. "Go over without a drink, and he'll offer to buy you one."

She had a point. That sorted, the girls flapped their hands at me, urging me to go off and find Jonathan. I made my way further into the room, but couldn't see him. He certainly wasn't where I'd last spotted him. Glancing back at the girls, I saw they were watching me like hawks. There was no escape; I'd have to keep looking. They would never allow me to go back over there with the excuse that I couldn't find him. With friends like mine, who needed enemies?

I scoured the room, which, with its dim lighting, wasn't the easiest thing to do. Finally, I saw him. He was feeding coins into the jukebox. Alone. Before I had chance to wimp out, I walked over to him. I had a quip on the tip of my tongue, ready.

I stood behind him and said, "I hope your taste in music has improved in the last five years!"

He jumped slightly, then turned around. He'd obviously recognised my voice straight away because he was grinning. "I thought it was you! How are you doing? You look great."

Before I could formulate a response, he'd wrapped me in a hug. He'd never been a skinny guy, but as I hugged him back and my face pressed against his chest, I could feel how solid he was.

There was pure muscle beneath his shirt. A delicious heat started to flicker between my legs.

I pulled back before I did something stupid, like allow my hands to stray towards his arse. The temptation was definitely there, especially as he *still* knew how to wear a pair of jeans. Over eight years after I'd first caught sight of that backside, it looked equally good. Possibly better, due to his bulkier frame.

"I'm good, thanks," I replied, still checking him out. "You look pretty good yourself."

It was true, too. Aside from the still-gorgeous arse and additional body mass, he looked good enough to eat. Working abroad obviously agreed with him. He carried a nice tan, and his hair was shorter. It suited him. I was pleased to note, though, that he still had his trademark facial hair. The times I'd fantasised about having it brush over certain parts of my body were too many to count.

I focused back on his face before my mind started wandering too much. He'd obviously seen my slightly dreamy expression, though, as a mischievous twinkle appeared in his blue eyes. God, I remembered that look. It inevitably meant trouble.

"So," I said brightly, trying desperately to deflect aforementioned trouble, "what are you doing here? I wasn't expecting to see you; last I heard, you were working over in Dubai."

"I was," he said, then took a sip of his drink. "I mean, I am. I'm home for a little while on holiday, and it was just lucky that it coincided with tonight. Who are you here with?"

"Very lucky. It's nice to see you. I'm here with the girls."

"Oh, they're here, too? Awesome. Hey, have you got a

drink?"

"No, I was just going to get one when I spotted you," I lied.

"I'll get you one. What are you having?"

"Double vodka and Coke, no ice, please."

His dimples appeared. "Some things never change. I'll be back in a mo'."

I watched him walk towards the bar. Or maybe "studied him intently" would be a better turn of phrase. It seemed his ability to bring out the total perv in me hadn't waned. Turning to the jukebox, in case he turned around and caught me checking him out, I noticed he still had a couple of credits left. Ha, more fool him for leaving me unattended with jukebox credits! I punched in the codes for a couple of my favourite songs and giggled to myself.

The girls had obviously stopped harassing the poor barman because it didn't take Jonathan long to come back with our drinks. I accepted mine with a smile and a thank you. I took a gulp of my drink, hoping to calm my still-jangling nerves. "So," I said, not wanting to let the silence last any longer, "how are things out in Dubai? Are you married yet?"

I spoke the words in a jovial tone, but I was really hoping he wasn't.

He wrinkled his nose. "God, no! I don't even have a girlfriend. I move around so much that I don't have the opportunity to get to know anybody. I'm not bothered at the moment, though; I enjoy what I do so I just take each day as it comes."

"Seems like a sound philosophy to me," I replied.

"And what about you? You still with that, um—"

"No, that finished ages ago. It's just little old me. To be fair, I'm so busy at the moment that I don't really have time for a relationship. I just started my own business."

Jonathan raised an eyebrow. "Well, that's a first."

I frowned. "What?"

"Us being single at the same time."

God, he was right. My heart pounded. "Hmm." I didn't trust myself to give a verbal response, mainly because I didn't know what he was getting at; if anything. The last thing I wanted was to get the wrong impression and make an idiot of myself.

Jonathan looked a little puzzled, but then we were saved from a potentially awkward conversation by my taste in music. I'd always been teased at uni—and not just by Jonathan—about the crap I had on my iPod. So, when one of my all-time favourite cheesy songs started blaring out, a collective groan went up.

Jonathan rolled his eyes. "Was this your doing?"

I gave a one-shouldered shrug. "Your fault. You shouldn't have left me unattended by the jukebox, especially when you had credits left!"

Slapping his hand theatrically to his forehead, he said, "I should have known it would be my fault."

I chuckled. Then his next move took me completely by surprise. After downing the rest of his drink and putting his empty glass on the table, he said, "May I have this dance?"

Given the song was cheesy pop, his offer wasn't as romantic as it sounded. Still, I wasn't going to waste the opportunity—both to dance to my favourite song and to potentially cop a feel—so I finished my own drink and took his proffered hand.

This was no sexy slow dance; we weren't even touching. But, after a couple of minutes of bopping around, we realised how silly we were being and started laughing. I was almost doubled over at one point, and when I looked back up, my mirth instantly disappeared.

Jonathan was looking at me with such a serious expression that I thought something was wrong. "What's up?"

He said nothing, grabbing my hands and pulling me to him. My blood was already thundering through my veins as a result of the attempted dancing and subsequent giggling, so it was a wonder the sudden proximity didn't make me explode.

The look in his eyes was earnest, his expression serious. "I still want you, you know."

Then he kissed me. There was no messing around—well, apart from the previous eight years, of course—he just leaned down and pressed his lips to mine. Without a thought about public displays of affection, I slipped my arms around his waist and kissed him back, opening my mouth to admit his tongue.

It was incredible. The culmination of eight years of sexual tension and unexplored feelings. My pussy juices dampened my thong, and Jonathan's cock pressed insistently against my stomach. If I'd have been someone else looking at us, I'd have been telling us to "get a room".

After a few seconds, I became horribly aware of the fact other people were probably thinking just that. I pulled away from the kiss, then stood on tiptoes to reach Jonathan's ear. "Is everyone staring at us?" I didn't dare look around to see if anyone was giving us disapproving glares.

"No," he replied, his arms still encircling my waist. "I don't think anybody noticed."

"Phew. I had visions of people shouting at us to get a room!" I laughed, then stopped abruptly when he spoke.

"Well, why don't we?"

It all happened so quickly I didn't register much of what was said on the way to find an empty room. Suddenly, he tried a door, mercifully found it unlocked, then pulled me into the room behind him.

Once the door was shut—and locked—after us, Jonathan stepped towards me, put his hands on my hips and bent to kiss me again. He pushed me backwards until my back was pressed against the door, his lips never losing contact with mine. His tongue explored my mouth, and his stubble grazed my skin, prompting old memories of me fantasising about how said facial hair would feel between my thighs. I moaned and grabbed his arse, pulling him tightly into my body. His erection strained against the material of his jeans.

Some unspoken command seemed to pass between us, and things picked up a pace. Jonathan's mouth left mine and started to trail down my face and neck, leaving kisses and nibbles in its wake. At the same time, he slipped his hands under my top and began to slide them up my stomach. When he reached the bottom of my bra, he continued, palming my lace-covered breasts and moaning against my neck as he felt their weight.

After flipping the cups of my bra down, Jonathan swept his hands over my already stiff nipples, making them ache for more. He moved back up and caught my lips in another toe-curling kiss and, at the same time, pinched my nipples. I groaned and arched my back, wanting the same friction—any friction—against my clit. My pussy was soaked, and I desperately needed him to touch me there.

Although our encounter had been a hell of a long time in coming and I didn't want it to be over too soon, my body didn't care. Jonathan was obviously being led by his cock rather than his brain, too, as he broke our kiss and yanked my top off, before dropping it at our feet. My bra soon followed. Then he kicked off his shoes and fumbled with his socks. I followed suit, then watched as he undid his shirt. The only light in the room came from the panel of glass above the door into the corridor. But it was enough. As he revealed his body, my mouth and cunt grew wetter.

He was toned and obviously spent time out of doors, topless. I was still staring when he discarded his shirt and looked at me. He grinned then nodded towards my jeans, at the same time popping open the top button of his fly. I mimicked him. He undid the next button. I had no more buttons, only a zip. I pulled it down slowly, teasingly, staring defiantly into his eyes as I did so. Finally, I parted the material to reveal my thong, which, by happy coincidence, was sexy.

Jonathan obviously thought so, too, as his eyes were glued to it. After a few seconds of staring, he suddenly undid the remaining buttons of his jeans and started to wriggle out of them, finally dropping them to the floor and kicking them away. His black boxers were tight and clearly stretched from the pressure of his cock, which, from what I could see, looked pretty sizeable.

He hooked his thumbs into the waistband and pulled the underwear down. His erection sprang free, pointing proudly up towards his bellybutton from an obviously well-maintained cluster of pubic hair. Precum already glistened on his glans, and I had the sudden urge to wrap my lips around his cock and taste him.

Instead, I pulled my jeans and knickers down in one go. Moving away from the door, I stepped towards Jonathan and tilted my head back for a kiss. He obliged, and as our lips met, our hands got busy. I wrapped my fingers around his thick shaft and began to stroke it, enjoying the velvety warmth in my hand. Returning the favour, Jonathan's fingers slipped between my pussy lips and met with sticky heat. We devoured each other's mouths hungrily, him sinking his teeth into my bottom lip as I tightened my grip on his cock.

I pushed my hips towards him, desperately needing to feel his touch on my clit. He took the hint, sliding further up my vulva and finally giving me friction where I most needed it. He made small but firm circles around the distended nub of nerve endings, and I gasped and moaned into his mouth then finally went silent as my climax hit.

My cunt greedily grabbed at nothing, and I cried out as the pleasure rolled over me in intense waves. Jonathan bent and picked me up just before I went limp. He carried me over to a desk, depositing me gently down before going over to rummage in his jeans. As my heart rate and breathing started to slow, I heard the distinct sound of a condom packet being torn open.

I opened my eyes and started to raise myself up on my elbows, but before I got there, Jonathan was back. Without warning, he grabbed my ankles and pulled me so my arse was at the edge of the desk. Parting my thighs, he gazed hungrily at my wetness for a few seconds before stepping between my legs and stroking his length up and down my vulva.

I moaned as his cock bumped against my still-sensitive clit. God, I needed him. I raised my backside, and Jonathan took the hint, sinking into me in one swift movement. I was so wet that his cock met with zero resistance, and soon, his balls rested against my arse. We stared at each other wide-eyed. I scarcely believed it was finally happening for us, and by the look on Jonathan's face, I suspected he felt the same.

After a couple of seconds, he began to move. I wrapped my legs around his back and with each of his forward movements, I pulled him tightly into me, crushing his pubic bone almost painfully against mine. As delicious as my first orgasm had been, I was greedy for another. At the rate we were going, I knew it wouldn't be far away.

I held on for as long as I could, letting Jonathan pick the pace and simply enjoying the incredible feeling of his cock pounding my pussy. After a while, he sped up of his own accord, and the faster he went, the rougher I wanted it. I encouraged him with my body, thrusting up to meet him, and with my words; releasing a torrent of obscenities.

Soon, I teetered on the edge. "Jon," I said, struggling to form coherent words, "I'm gonna... unh... come."

Muttering something even more incoherent back at me, he gripped my hips tightly and began to fuck me for all he was worth, bouncing me on his shaft like a ragdoll. My cunt began to twitch and, seconds later, I screamed my release, not caring who might hear. Jonathan followed closely behind, digging his fingers into my flesh as he came, grunting and moaning expletives. Then he slumped over me, supporting his weight on one arm and resting his head on my chest. My heart pounded against his cheek.

We lay silently for a while, until his softening cock slipped from me. Then he stood and turned his back to me. I heard the snap of rubber and the rustling of paper. He'd dropped it in the wastepaper basket.

I laughed. "I feel sorry for the person who's got to empty that bin."

"Me too, but I'll be thousands of miles away by Monday, so I don't give a shit!"

We looked at each other silently as his words hung in the air. They'd been blasé, but they'd hit us both hard.

He came and sat back next to me, then pulled me into his arms. "Fuck, Lauren," he murmured into my hair, "what are we going to do?"

In that moment, I realised that, far from tying up our loose ends, we'd simply created a much bigger tangle we'd have to unpick before we'd get our happy ending. But I knew with every part of my being that he was worth it, so I simply replied, "We'll work it out."

Delivering the Goods

It was one hell of an extravagance. But she had a *damn* good reason: she was horny.

There was absolutely nothing stopping Michelle from jumping in the car and going to the supermarket herself. Nothing except her horniness and the resulting barmy idea.

The delivery driver might not even be male, let alone someone she'd want to fuck. Michelle decided to take a chance. She reached for the computer mouse and clicked 'Place Order.' She mentally noted her delivery slot—between 2 and 4 p.m. That gave her hours to prepare.

Michelle ran a bubble bath, then got in for a good long soak to soften her skin and relax her muscles. She shaved her legs, underarms and pussy. She soaped up from neck to toe, then rinsed. Finally, she washed her hair. Satisfied she was clean and smooth, Michelle got out of the bath and pulled the plug, dried off, then padded through the flat to her bedroom.

Once there, she retrieved a pot of body butter from her supplies and massaged it into her skin from the neck downwards, smiling as she breathed in the delicate yet tempting scent. After applying a posh moisturiser to her face, Michelle turned her attention to her hair.

Should she go with straight and sleek, or curly and wild? Chances were the guy—if indeed it was a guy—wouldn't notice either way. But since her mood was impulsive, wild, she figured her hair should match.

Her grooming complete, she dressed with equal care and

attention, then settled herself on the sofa with a book. Daytime TV never was much good at the weekend, plus her erotic novel would keep her libido simmering until the buzzer went, announcing the arrival of her shopping. And her shag. Hopefully.

She desperately tried not to think about the many ways in which her crazy plan could fail. It didn't work. Her mind flitted through the possibilities: the driver could be a woman, gay, faithful, in a rush, not interested, too old, too young… the list went on.

Perhaps this wasn't such a great idea. Feeling a little glum, Michelle forced herself to concentrate on her smutty book. *There's nothing like a bit of erotica to cheer a girl up.* Soon, she was drawn into the story and, totally absorbed, didn't notice the time tick along. In fact, she didn't notice *anything* outside of those pages until the rumble of an engine reached her ears. With a gasp she marked her page, abandoned the book, and rushed to the window to see the supermarket delivery van pulling up.

Michelle held her breath as she squinted at the driver. The angle of the sun meant the van's cab was cast in shadow. Damn it. *Come on, hurry up!*

Finally, the driver's door swung open and the occupant got out. Michelle's heart pounded as she waited for him or her to appear at the back of the van, where she'd have a perfect view. Oh my God, there he was!

Michelle pressed herself against the windowpane, desperate to get a better look. He was tall and well-built, both characteristics she was a fan of. Unfortunately, he wore a woolly hat which meant that even as he turned towards the building she couldn't see much else. So; tall and well-built, check. Everything else, well, she'd just have to wait. But only a matter of minutes…

As the sound of the buzzer shrilled through the flat, Michelle forced herself to remain calm. The last thing she needed was to come across as desperate. She sauntered over and pressed the intercom button which would allow her to speak with the driver.

"Hello? I'm here with your grocery delivery."

Add sexy voice to the list of attributes. "Great! Come on up."

She buzzed him into the building, then waited for the sound of the doorbell. She didn't have to wait long—*the lift is obviously working today.*

Michelle took a deep breath. *This is it. Now or never.* She opened up.

A sex god stood in the corridor. The stereotypical tall, dark and handsome bloke you normally only saw on the front of magazines. *What the fuck is he doing working as a delivery driver? He should be a model.*

Michelle mentally shook herself. "Hi!" she practically sang, then inwardly berated herself. The man would think she was a moron. *Just calm down, you daft cow.*

She cleared her throat and stepped aside. "Please, come in. Could you possibly pop the stuff on the work surface? Can I get you a drink?"

"No problem," he said, dumping the box where Michelle had requested, "and do you know what, I wouldn't say no to a quick drink, if that's all right. I don't normally, but it's been manic today—I haven't even had a lunch break!"

Michelle saw her golden opportunity, and grasped it with both hands. She closed the door and crossed over to him. "In that case, would you like a sandwich? I'm pretty peckish myself… sorry, I didn't get your name."

"I'm Darren." He held out his hand, and she shook it.

"Michelle." His skin was smooth and warm to the touch. Michelle could well imagine how good those hands would feel on her body… She subtly glanced towards his other hand, searching for signs of a wedding ring, and saw none. *Excellent.*

"No I'm fine, I wouldn't like to put you out."

"You're not. I just said I was hungry. It's no problem to make two instead of one. Honestly."

"If you're sure?"

Michelle gestured for him to sit down at the breakfast bar. He dutifully pulled out a stool and sat, watching her prepare their snack.

They chatted idly whilst she worked, Michelle checking up what ingredients he wanted in his sandwich, and what he wanted to drink, amongst other things. Darren dutifully answered her questions, and responded with a few of his own.

"I've never delivered to you before, and this is my regular area. I'm just curious—why the sudden change? Or have you just moved in here?"

Caught unawares, Michelle wasn't quite sure how to respond. She decided to go for the honesty tack. Well, almost honest. "I'm on my own, and I hate supermarket shopping. All those crowds and kids having tantrums drive me mad. It's just easier to do it all online—no pushing, shoving and queuing, and a lovely gentleman brings your goods right to the door. What more could any woman want?"

She whisked his plate and glass of juice over to the breakfast bar, and accidentally-on-purpose brushed her breast against his arm as she put them in front of him, lingering longer than was strictly necessary.

"Th-thanks." Darren immediately grabbed the glass and took a huge gulp of juice.

Michelle smirked as she turned to grab her own lunch, then returned and sat next to him at the bar. She watched from beneath her eyelashes as he bit into his sandwich; his long, graceful fingers bringing the morsel to his mouth, his luscious lips parting to accommodate it. How she'd love to be on the receiving end of...

"...delicious."

"Wha—?" Michelle was shaken from her daydream as he spoke.

"The sandwich." He frowned. "I said it's delicious."

"Oh, thanks. Want some dessert when you're done?"

She regretted the words almost as soon as they were out of her mouth. This could go one of three ways; he could take her literally—in which case he'd be disappointed as she never kept anything in, or he could pick up the double entendre and run for the hills, or he could pick up the double entendre and run for the bedroom. She sincerely hoped for the latter.

Darren raised an eyebrow. "What's on offer?"

She flashed what she hoped was a wicked grin. "Anything you like."

It was the most obvious come-on, but Darren grinned back,

his green eyes meeting hers, full of mischief.

Michelle hopped off her stool and headed for the bedroom, willing him to follow. Milliseconds later she heard his stool scraping against the floor as he pushed it back to join her.

Once in the bedroom, there was no mistaking their intent. They were adults; they knew the score. Michelle looked up at Darren with a seductive smile. He needed no other invitation—he reached out and tangled his hands into her hair, then pulled her close for a kiss. She responded by winding her arms around his neck and melding her lower body to his. Darren was already erect and raring to go.

"You know," he said, between kisses, "you're my last drop-off today."

"Really?" Michelle grinned widely as she tugged off his sweater and began attacking the buttons on his shirt. "Well then, that means we have all the time in the world, doesn't it? We can have some real fun."

"*Real* fun, eh?" He went to work undoing her jeans. "And what does that involve?"

"Get all your clothes off and you'll find out."

Minutes later, they were naked but for their underwear and kissing heatedly on the bed. Michelle snaked a hand down to cup Darren's cock through his boxer shorts—still rock hard, and red hot to boot. *Time for a closer look.*

Her hormones raging, she pushed Darren onto his back, then wriggled down the bed. Eagerly, she grasped the waistband of his boxers and manoeuvred them off him to reveal an impressive hard on. She all but drooled as she gazed at his lovely cock, long and thick, already oozing precum.

Michelle stuck her tongue into the sticky stuff seeping from the end of his cock, relishing Darren's resultant moan. Then she took him into her mouth, sliding down and swallowing as much of him as was possible. She wrapped her fingers around the base of his shaft and began to stroke him slowly as she gulped and slurped. Appreciative noises came from somewhere above her head, so Michelle continued. She'd waited long enough for this, so she was going to make the most of it.

By now her pussy was dripping wet in anticipation of being filled to the hilt by this man's cock. Her underwear was sticking to her, so she figured now was as good a time as any to take them off. After shimmying out of her thong, Michelle threw it at Darren's head, momentarily pulling away from his cock and giggling as it landed directly over his eyes.

"No," she ordered as he went to remove it, "that was such a good shot that it's gotta stay there now."

Amused and aroused all at once, she crawled up his taut, muscular body and planted a kiss on his lips. As he responded, his cock tapped against her stomach, no doubt missing the attention. She couldn't make him wait any longer—or herself, if she was being truthful. She hastily grabbed a condom from her bedside drawer, tore it open and rolled it on him. Then, with no warning, she mounted his cock. She slid down firmly until he was completely embedded in her, eliciting a moan from Darren. Kissing him again, she remained stationary on his cock as she adjusted to being filled so completely.

It had been a while. Then she began to ride him.

Afraid of smashing their mouths together as she picked up the pace, Michelle broke their kiss and sat upright. She whipped the knickers off his face and threw them off to one side—very glad she had once saw the expression of bliss on his face. Probably hers had a similar look.

Her pussy throbbed and tingled. She reached down to give her clit some attention, rubbing it as Darren grasped her arse cheeks and pulled her onto him, meeting her bounces with upward thrusts. Their movements became more frenzied, and the tell-tale signs of her climax made themselves known. Darren reached up to cup her breasts, then pinched and tugged at her nipples.

The delicious sensations built up inside her, and she stroked her clit for all it was worth. Seconds later her walls spasmed around Darren's cock, the waves growing stronger as her orgasm hit fully. His shaft swelled and then exploded inside her, milked relentlessly by her pulsating core.

When their cries had quietened, and their heaving chests and thundering pulses had slowed, Michelle rolled off Darren and propped herself up on her elbow. Then she gazed over at him, a plan beginning to form. "So you deliver to this area all the time, then, you said?"

"Yeah," he said, frowning. "Why do you ask?"

"Oh," she smirked, "just wondering…"

In the Frame

As soon as the teacher, lecturer, course leader—what *did* you call someone who was teaching a class for adults, anyway?—entered the room, all of Gina's misgivings about signing up for the photography class disappeared. If the worst came to the absolute worst and she didn't learn a damn thing, then at least she'd have enough fantasy fodder to keep her going for months.

He was *gorgeous*. Dressed in a smart casual manner, in dark blue jeans and a white T-shirt, along with funky Converse trainers, he'd got the outfit down. And the man *inside* the outfit was perfection, too. Shorter than her usual type, he made up for it with his slightly messy spiky black hair, startling blue-green eyes and scruff which clearly hadn't decided whether it wanted to become a full-on beard or not.

Gina was deeply in lust. And he hadn't uttered a word yet.

When he did, her hormones ratcheted up.

"Hi everyone, I'm Chris, your course leader. We'll be working together the next few weeks to improve your photography skills."

His voice was deep and gravelly, but not ridiculously so. Just enough to set off a dull ache low in Gina's belly.

Come on, Gina, get a fucking grip! You're not a thirteen-year-old schoolgirl with a crush on the teacher. You're thirty-two years old, a grown woman with plenty of experience under your belt. A mere mortal man shouldn't be affecting you this way.

Except he was, and unless she pulled herself together, she was going to make a complete twat of herself. She busied herself with getting her camera out of her bag. Glancing around the room, she saw that there was as much variety to the cameras as there was to the students. It was part of the reason she'd signed up for the course, which had promised to improve photography skills, even if one was only using a camera on a mobile phone. It wasn't about having huge SLRs with lenses longer than her leg, or all the latest gadgets—it was about going back to basics. Which was to be expected, for a beginner's course.

Having gotten her errant hormones under some semblance of control, Gina tried to focus on what Chris was saying, staring intently at the examples that were being beamed from his laptop to the whiteboard.

He was good. *Really* good. Of course, the photos would have been taken using the best cameras, by an expert, then improved even further with editing software. Obviously they were going to be a damn sight better than anything she could achieve. But it didn't matter—she wasn't going for any prizes, or an exhibition. She'd just wanted a hobby, and thought photography would compliment her love of the outdoors. Her shots would be for personal use, maybe bunged on Facebook and Pinterest. So if she completed this six week introductory course with a better grasp of the basics, then she'd have achieved her goal.

And if she could manage that without melting into a pathetic puddle of girl goo at the feet of the gorgeous course leader, then all the better.

"Right," Chris said brightly, "that's enough waffling for now. Shall we head into the gardens and get some shots? We'll have half an hour out there, then come back up here and discuss what we did well, and what we could have done better."

There were murmurs of agreement, and the students filed out of the room. Chris locked the door before leading them through the college building and out into the lovely grounds that nestled between it and the river.

That was the biggest bonus to running such courses in the summer, Gina figured; plenty of hours of daytime, and excellent light. Even her untrained eye could see they'd get some great photographs, with sunbeams peeking through the leaves and branches of the trees, dappling the grass and the plants.

Putting some distance between herself and Chris, she switched on her camera and began snapping away, each time trying to pay care and attention to what she was doing, framing images, rather than just pointing and clicking. Even by her own standards she was capturing some pretty good stuff.

She was crouching in a rather awkward position to get a photograph through the branches of a bush when a voice came from behind her. "That's great! One of my pieces of advice is to get creative with your positioning, not just taking photos from eye level."

Trying to remain cool as Chris's seductive tones seeped in through her ears and sent sparks through her entire body, Gina pretended to ignore him for a moment, took a couple of photos, then attempted to stand. Unfortunately, her cool factor failed entirely when her knees made an unpleasant popping sound. Wincing, Gina tumbled onto the grass on her arse, landing with an "Umph!" and immediately wishing a hole would open up in said grass and swallow her.

"Oh, shit!" Chris said, stepping over to her and holding out a hand. "Are you all right? Let me help you up. I'm so sorry, I didn't mean to distract you."

Having no other option, she grasped his hand and allowed him to pull her to her feet. Heat radiated from her face so ferociously she feared she'd give him sunburn. "Thanks," she muttered, then turned her attention to her camera, hoping it hadn't been damaged in the fall.

Fortunately, it seemed to be okay. Glancing back up, she saw Chris was still there.

"Are you all right?" His eyes were full of concern, reminding her that although he looked like a god on earth, he was, in fact, human.

"Yesss," she said on an exhale. "Just dying of embarrassment, that's all."

"Well, at least you're dying for your art. What better way to go, eh?" He grinned, deep dimples in each cheek simply serving to finish her off. Scratch months; she was going to be fantasising about this guy for *years*.

"Yeah," she replied, managing a small smile. *Well done, Gina. Wow him with your conversational prowess.*

"I really am sorry. Let me make it up to you?" He lowered his voice, though no one was nearby. "Buy you a drink after class?"

"Mmm-hmm!" she said, the enthusiasm apparent in her tone, despite the fact she hadn't managed an actual word. *Idiot.*

"Great," Chris replied, not seeming to notice her lunacy. "Wait for me, yeah? But not, um, in an obvious way. I don't think I can get sacked for going for drinks with my students, but I don't want to risk it. Probably looks quite unprofessional—especially on the first session."

"Yup. Understood."

The rest of the session couldn't go quickly enough. After Chris headed off to see some of the other students, she brushed herself down, hoping she didn't have grass stains on her backside.

Later, the group filed out of the room, calling their goodbyes, and Gina deliberately took her time tidying her things away into her bag. She stood, and, when the second-to-last student had left the room, she said quietly, "Shall I wait for you in the car park?"

She shuffled towards the door as she waited for his answer.

When it came, it wasn't what she'd expected. "I want you to wait right here."

What? So they weren't going for a drink?

After poking his head out of the door to make sure everyone was gone, he leaned back in, closed it, and locked it. Then, crossing over to her, he carefully removed her handbag and keys from her hands, and placed them on the nearest desk.

A part of Gina's brain knew exactly where Chris's behaviour was leading. But the rest of it was a bundle of confusion. *What? Me? Seriously? But we've only just met. He doesn't even know me...*

The whirling dervish of thoughts halted instantly when he grabbed her wrists and pulled her flush against him. "I didn't get this wrong, did I?" he whispered, his breath hot against her cheek, the

light scent of mint invading her nostrils. "Gina," he insisted.
"Answer me, please. You haven't said much, but I kinda thought
there was something between us... and I thought here was a better
place to discuss it than a crowded pub."

Discuss? What was there to discuss? She wanted him, and
apparently the feeling was mutual. The evidence of that was pressing
insistently against her stomach, obvious despite the layers of
clothing between them.

"No," she said, gaining control of her voice again. "You
didn't get it wrong."

The whoosh of breath and the chuckle that followed
indicated his relief. "And you're, um, available?"

"Yes. Are you?"

"Yes."

She believed him. She didn't know why, but she did. "Well
then," her hormones, which had made her so tongue-tied before, now
made her bold, "what else is there to discuss? I like you, you like
me, we're both single, let's fuck."

This time, his laugh was a little high-pitched. "Um, well,
when you put it like that... but, let me buy you a drink some other
time?"

So he didn't just want to fuck and run. Excellent; but they'd
figure all that out later. Right now, she wanted him inside her. The
arousal that had been burning inside her since the beginning of the
class had increased to fever pitch, and her body was overwhelming
her mind.

"Yes, okay," she said impatiently, reaching down to stroke

his cock through his jeans, "but now... I want you." She reached for her bag and retrieved a condom from the inside pocket.

"Here." She shoved the packet at him, then undid her jeans and shoved them and her knickers down around her ankles. Unladylike, perhaps, but time was of the essence. She couldn't remember the last time she'd felt this desperate need for a man, this urgency. Her cunt was slick; juices coated her inner thighs.

Turning, she shuffled to the nearest desk and bent over it, looking over her shoulder. Chris had released and sheathed his cock. More wetness seeped from her core at the sight of him; hard, thick and long, perfect for the task ahead.

"Please," she begged, "fuck me."

"But we haven't even kissed," he protested, moving up behind her and raking his hands over her naked flesh.

A shiver ran through her at his touch. "I know. But... later."

Apparently unable to resist any longer, Chris put tentative fingertips to her labia, and, finding her soaked, let out a guttural groan. The fingertips were quickly replaced by his cock, which he rubbed up and down her seam a couple of times, before pressing between her swollen lips. He entered her easily, and groaned again as her hot, wet cunt gobbled him up.

Sounds tumbled from Gina's lips, too, as Chris's shaft stretched her. Damn, he felt good. And when he reached around and began playing with her rapidly growing clit, he felt *amazing*. God... it wasn't going to take long for her to come, probably because, in her mind at least, they'd been indulging in foreplay ever since the start of the class. Now she was primed, ready to explode all over his delicious dick, which was thrusting slow but deep inside her.

And, following a couple more strokes from those skilful fingers, she did just that. She bit down on her fist as her orgasm hit with force, sending powerful waves crashing through her and causing her internal walls to grip and spasm around him.

Squeezing her eyes tightly shut as she rode out the climax, she felt Chris come, his cock swelling further before beginning a spasm of its own, shooting jet after jet of spunk into the condom. His muttered expletives made her smile, as did the endorphins flooding her bloodstream.

Wow, that had been completely out of the blue... but who cared? It had been *fantastic.*

As Chris slumped over her back, breathing heavily, Gina had no doubt she'd be signing up for more than just the intermediary photography class.

Private Performance

It wasn't at all surprising that Robyn's hormones were on overdrive. She *was* watching London's most popular male dance troupe, after all. As well as being incredibly talented, they were also super sexy. Their rabid fans followed them everywhere, battling for front row seats, screaming and waving throughout shows, then dashing outside afterwards, hoping to catch the men leaving so they could beg for autographs and selfies. They were as obsessive as the fans of boy bands, maybe more so. Robyn got it, totally, but she wasn't quite in that league. Not outwardly, anyway.

She, too, followed the group everywhere she possibly could, spending her hard-earned cash on the best tickets money could buy. For once, she was glad to be a City banker, meaning she could afford it without having to worry about paying her bills and mortgage.

What made her different, though, was her behaviour post-performance. She didn't head backstage or outside, hoping to get up close and personal with the boys. Instead, she dashed straight home and masturbated herself into blissful oblivion over thoughts of a single member of the group. Sean Rudd. She'd lost count of the number of orgasms she'd had while fantasising about him.

Her feelings for him could definitely be counted as obsessive. Ever since she'd first seen the group—after being dragged unwillingly by some work friends—she'd been hooked on Sean. She wasn't even sure why. He wasn't the best-looking of the group, though of course he was far from ugly. There was just something about him, and given she'd never been that close—no closer than the front row, anyway—to him, let alone spoken to him, she couldn't put her finger on it.

The way he moved was undoubtedly a huge turn-on; she'd always had a thing for men who could dance, and in the absence of Justin Timberlake, Sean took the number one fantasy spot. But then, all five of the guys danced brilliantly. And they were all good-looking, with great bodies. So why Sean?

The thought bugged Robyn on and off throughout the show. She studied each man in turn, then allowed her gaze to remain on her personal favourite. The group's perfectly choreographed moves brought them close to the front of the stage. Sean caught her eye and winked. Robyn was grateful the spotlights weren't on her as an intense heat washed over her face, then zipped straight down her body and to her groin.

It was then she got it. The reason that—for her, at least—Sean stood out.

It was all in the attitude. He had raw sex appeal. The other guys—although good—looked as though to them it was literally just a job. They had no massive love for what they were doing and were probably just trying to earn enough money to get them through university. Sean, however, was a bit older than the others. Perhaps he, too, had started dancing to pay for an education but had discovered he liked it so much that he didn't want to leave. Whatever the reason, Robyn was incredibly glad he was there.

She stared unashamedly at him as he moved around the stage, muscles flexing, arse wiggling, and a big grin on his face. He looked damn good, and as though he was having the time of his life. Provocative steps as part of the routine had the crowd screaming—

heaven knows what would happen if the boys took any more clothes off—and Sean loved it. Loved the attention, the adoration. He lapped it up like a cat with a large bowl of the finest cream.

The idea of lapping, and cream, sent Robyn's mind into the gutter. Thoughts of Sean spreading her legs and eating her eager pussy filled her mind to the point that everything else faded away. The screaming women, the thumping music, the electric atmosphere. It was all gone, except for him. She continued to watch him bopping around the stage, getting mildly irritated when any of the other guys got in front of him. Soon, though, she had the most perfect view— better than she could ever have hoped for.

He was right in front of her. And just as their routine became particularly sexed-up, too. Robyn thought she'd died and gone to heaven, especially when he started thrusting his hips in her direction. She was vaguely aware of the screams of the women around her growing louder, and if it was even possible, shriller. She resisted the temptation to cover her ears.

Her mouth grew drier by the second as she watched him. She felt like a starving man at a buffet as she drank in the sight before her eyes; his grinning face, mischievous blue eyes, sweat-slicked dark hair, delicious torso, smooth but for the slim line of hair running from his bellybutton and down into the waistband of his tiny shorts. Her gaze didn't go any further south than his shorts, however; his bulging crotch did a damn good job of keeping her attention. That was until suddenly his face appeared in the area she'd been gawping at. He was crouching down and beckoning to her.

She shook her head; there was no way she wanted to be

dragged up onto the stage. It just wasn't her style. But then, it wasn't the group's style, either. She'd certainly never seen them do it before, not even for hen parties. He gestured at her again, more urgently this time. After grabbing her glass and taking a large gulp of wine for courage, she slid out of her seat and took a couple of steps forward to the edge of the stage. A nearby security guard watched her, clearly making sure she wasn't going to go crazy and jump on Sean or something. When she was close enough, he put his fingers on her chin and gently turned her head before whispering something into her ear. Then he gave her a little shove back to her seat and carried on with his routine.

When she reached her chair, she practically collapsed into it. She could hardly believe what he'd said. Looking at the contents of the table, she wondered if she might have consumed enough wine that she was drunk and therefore imagining the whole thing. She wasn't—she was still on her first glass and only a little over halfway through it.

So he *had* said what she thought he'd said—hadn't he? Because she *thought* he'd asked her to come to his dressing room after the show. She shook her head in disbelief and looked back up to the stage. The next time her gaze met Sean's, he winked again and gave her a smile that reached from ear to ear, and then a couple of extra hip thrusts.

She gasped. So she *hadn't* imagined it.

Backstage after the show it was then. To his dressing room, no less.

Shit.

The rest of the performance passed in a blur of gleaming muscles and flashing lights. As the group headed off the stage following their encore, Sean was last. He turned to look at her, then nodded his head in the direction of the door that led backstage and gave her a thumbs-up. He was gone before she could react.

Soon afterwards the lights came up and people started filing out of the room. The avid fans were already hurrying to the back door of the building. The rest, presumably, were going home or heading on to a bar or something. That left Robyn, sitting at the front of the room, all by herself. The security guard who had eyeballed her earlier cleared his throat, startling her.

She gave him a wry smile, then downed the rest of her wine. In a daze, she grabbed her stuff, then forced herself to put one foot in front of the other and go in search of Sean. She felt like a giddy teenager going on her first date, or anticipating her first kiss. Possibly both.

She passed through the door and emerged into a dimly-lit corridor, then made her way down it, looking at each door as she passed. The boys weren't exactly A-listers, so their names were written on pieces of A4 paper and stuck to the relevant dressing room doors. Glamorous it was not, but Robyn didn't care. All she was bothered about at that particular moment was the fact she was about to meet the man she'd been lusting over for the past few months. She could hardly believe it, and part of her wanted to turn and run, and not stop until she was back at home with the door locked firmly behind her. But of course if she did that, she'd regret it until her dying day, so she located the door with Sean's name on it, and knocked.

"Come in!"

Following a brief pause to smooth her hair and attempt to stop the tremble in her hands, Robyn opened the door and stepped into the room.

Sean turned from where he was packing things into a small suitcase and smiled at her. He'd changed out of his stage outfit and thrown on a T-shirt and tracksuit bottoms. Presumably he planned to have a shower when he got home, wherever that was. She wondered if she was about to find out.

"Hey," he said, crossing the room towards her. He pushed the door closed, then turned to face her. "I'm glad you came. I didn't know if you would."

"Y-yes, I'm here." Talk about stating the bloody obvious. She needed to suck her nerves up before she made a complete and utter fool of herself.

He laughed softly. "So, are you going to tell me your name?"

"Oh! Sorry. I'm Robyn." She stuck her hand out. He took it, but then instead of shaking it, he pressed a kiss to her knuckles. Robyn giggled girlishly.

"It's nice to meet you, Robyn. But now, you must excuse my forwardness, but the minibus will be leaving in about twenty minutes. I invited you here because you've been at nearly all of our shows in London, and unless I'm quite mistaken, you've been watching me, in particular. Josh and Mike are the ones who usually have the ladies' attention—but you don't look at them nearly as much as you look at me. And what I want to know is: why?"

Robyn opened her mouth, then closed it again. She wasn't quite sure how to word what she wanted to say without sounding like a crazy stalker. But then, *she* didn't hang around outside the stage doors after each show. So maybe she wasn't as stalkerish as the other women. Certainly Sean wouldn't have invited her back here if he thought she was some kind of threat.

Figuring she had nothing to lose, except perhaps a bit of pride, she bit the bullet. "Um, well, it's because I love to watch you. Dancing, I mean. It's so sexy and it makes me really hot. The other guys are good, of course, but you're just in a whole other league." She shrugged, as if her words were no big deal.

Sean took a step closer to her, until he was right in her personal space. The scent of fresh sweat and cologne invaded Robyn's nostrils and sent a zing of arousal rushing to her groin. "So," he murmured, "why don't you wait outside like the others? They throw themselves at us, feel us up when we agree to have photos taken with them and all sorts."

Robyn shook her head, then blushed when she realised what she'd have to confess if she planned to be truthful with him. She decided to go for it. *You only live once.*

Her heart pounded. She gave a tight smile, then forced the words out before she lost her nerve. "I don't wait outside because I always rush home and, um, touch myself while thinking of you." She dropped her gaze to the floor, not wanting to see his reaction.

"Touch yourself?" He took her bag from her and placed it carefully down on a nearby table. Then he put his fingers beneath her jaw and lifted her head. "Touch yourself how?"

Robyn's cheeks flamed. As if it hadn't been bad enough telling him in the first place—now he wanted all the sordid details! She felt like a rabbit in the headlights as he stared at her, waiting for an answer. Her lips appeared to be stuck together. She couldn't open them, never mind get any words to come out.

Then, Sean removed the need for her to speak. He held her chin in place, then moved his other hand beneath her skirt and touched her pussy through her underwear. "Like this?" he said, cupping her mound and pressing the heel of his hand to her clit.

She couldn't nod, because of his grip on her chin. So she— barely—managed to whisper, "Y-yes." Then she gasped, because Sean started to rub her.

"Do you do this, too?"

Now she *did* nod, because he'd released her chin and wrapped his arm around her back, pulling her up against him. Their chests pressed together, and his breath tickled through her hair. Deftly, he pushed the crotch of her rapidly dampening thong to one side and touched her bare skin. She groaned, and immediately Sean traced his fingers up and down her slit, not dipping between the folds or so much as grazing against her clit.

Robyn rolled her hips, yearning for him to stroke her nub or to slip his thick fingers inside her.

He teased her for a little longer, until it appeared that he, too, couldn't wait any more. He manoeuvred his hand so his thumb pressed against her clit, then pushed a finger inside her saturated channel. Their combined moans filled the space around them, and Robyn grabbed Sean's biceps, purely for something to hold on to.

She didn't entirely trust her legs to hold her up.

"Good idea," he growled. "Hold on tight, babe, because I'm going to make you come."

With that, he pushed another finger inside her and curved them to press against her G-spot. Gasping, she craned her neck to watch what he was doing. Watch those talented fingers as they pleasured her, teased her to orgasm. She couldn't see much, of course, mainly the inside of his wrist, the heel of his hand and part of his thumb. But it was enough. When he moved a little, she glimpsed the shine of liquid on his palm. Her juices. That, coupled with the squishing sounds coming from her pussy, helped Robyn to picture a very erotic image, one that grew increasingly vivid the closer to climax she became.

And she was getting very close indeed. Her thighs stiffened, and a tremble ran through her as the delicious pressure grew in her abdomen. Its intensity increased, making her feel like a balloon—air continuing to pump into her, stretching her, until she was ready to pop.

Tingles combined with the pressure, and she dug her nails into Sean's arms as she teetered on the very edge, continuing to observe the busy hand between her legs. Then, with a flick of his wrist and thumb, she plummeted over the precipice. The trembles grew into shakes, and she arched her back as ecstasy overtook her body. She let out a scream, not caring who heard her.

Sean removed his hand and wrapped his other arm around her, pulling her into a hug and pressing a kiss to her head as she came down from her climax. He murmured sweet nothings into her hair and stroked her back; very intimate gestures for such a random encounter. But Robyn didn't mind. It was nice.

She snuggled into his embrace as she came back to herself, and soon felt the flames of her arousal building up once more. She was just about to disentangle herself from Sean and drop to her knees in order to repay the favour when a knock came at the door.

With a murmured apology, Sean pulled her skirt down and moved over to the door. He opened it a little, enough to speak to whoever was there without revealing who was in the room with him. A rushed conversation took place, then Sean nodded agreement and dismissed the person he'd been speaking to.

Turning to Robyn, he said, "You coming back to mine, then? There's room in the minivan for a little one."

Robyn grabbed her bag and, despite the tremble in her legs, hurried over to him. She'd had a taster of the man she'd been watching for months, now she was more than ready for a full-on private performance.

Deeper Underground

"So, where are we going again?" Emmy asked as she and her friend Charis exited London Bridge Tube station.

"It's called The London Bridge Experience and The London Tombs. It's basically two attractions in one, designed to scare the shit out of you."

"Fair enough." Emmy shrugged as they crossed the road. "Though I can't imagine it'll be any different to the London Dungeons."

"Probably not, but it'll be a laugh."

"That it will."

They reached the entrance and got into the queue, grinning as the costumed and made-up actors and actresses got the soon-to-be punters in the mood by walking up and down the length of the line, being all moody and menacing and trying to make people jump. It was too much for some, it seemed, as a bunch of folks left the queue without even going into the building.

"Wimps," Charis said, nudging Emmy and pointing at a family who had scuttled off, much to the dismay of the creepy-costume guy who'd frightened them. "I don't think he's supposed to scare customers so much they leave altogether!"

Emmy sniggered. "No, I'm sure he's not. But at least it means we're closer to the front of the queue now. I hope we don't freak out before we get there."

Snorting, Charis replied, "I doubt it. We're made of sterner stuff than that, aren't we?" She linked arms with her friend as they shuffled forward.

"Yeah, definitely. Hard as nails."

Suddenly there was some commotion and they could hear shouting, though not make out the words. Then the people in the line started repeating what had been said. Finally, the request made its way to them. "Oh, they're looking for two more people!" Emmy looked around. "I guess we should go—nobody else is. They must all be bigger groups."

"Okay, let's go." The two women made their way up to the front, where one of the ghoulish-looking staff indicated they should enter the building. They headed into the gloom, paid their money at the counter, then joined the back of the group that had already gone in. After a little preamble about health and safety and the fact that "the live actors will not touch you, so please do not touch them," they all filed into the next room.

In the darkness, Emmy and Charis stayed close to each other as the actors and actresses told spooky tales of London's bloody and unpleasant past—Queen Boudicca and the legions of Rome, King Olaf the Viking, William Wallace, the Black Death, the Great Fire of London, the Great Stink, Jack the Ripper, and much more. They were told that London Bridge's gatehouse displayed the heads of traitors, and that the Tombs were formerly a plague pit. As she exchanged a worried glance with her friend, Emmy came to the conclusion that the place, although just as theatrical as the London Dungeons, seemed to have an edge that made it creepier, somehow. This wasn't just stories—it was stuff that had really happened, and on the very spot on which they stood. And they hadn't even been into the actual Tombs yet.

"Okay, everyone!" said the member of staff currently in charge of freaking them out. "We're at the end of the first part of the experience now. Next, we're going into a room where you'll be divided into two groups, ready to begin your journey into the London Tombs. A journey from which you may never return!" A maniacal laugh filled the space, a door banged, and after a couple of shrieks, the group was herded forward.

They were notified this was the last point at which someone could change their mind. A member of staff would lead anyone out who didn't want to go into the Tombs, to wait for their friends and relatives in the gift shop. Emmy held back a snort—of course they'd be made to wait in the gift shop, in the hope they'd spend some money while they were there.

A few younger patrons immediately asked to be led out, and it was only when the rules and regulations were explained that Emmy's arm suddenly exploded in pain. Turning, she saw Charis's pale face reflected in the few lights in the room. "I've got to go," her friend whispered. "Single file, hands on shoulders—sounds like it's going to be claustrophobic. I can't be doing with that!"

"Oh, okay hon, let's go then. No problem. Hang on!" she called out. "Two more here."

"No, no," Charis said, shaking her head. "You stay. I don't want to ruin it for you. I'll just go back to the hotel and chill for a bit. Figure out where we can go for dinner. Somewhere delicious."

Emmy frowned. "Don't be silly, I'll come with you."

"Seriously, I insist. Stay. And then you can come back afterwards and tell me what a wimp I was."

"Only if you're sure."

"I'm sure. Now go, we're holding everyone up." She turned and hurried after the departing group, giving a little wave, and Emmy watched her warily for a couple of seconds before moving back towards those heading into the Tombs.

"Sorry," she said to everyone who was waiting. "I'm ready when everyone else is."

"Okay," the member of staff said, "just to recap—you're getting into a line. Prepare to put your hands on the shoulders of the person in front of you. Remember, you must not let go, you must not touch anything, or anyone, other than the person in front."

She nodded. "Right, got it."

Someone shuffled up behind her, and she glanced over her shoulder. A tall, broad man stood there—clearly the one who was brave enough to be at the back of the line. Deep down, she was kind of glad it wasn't her. In the dim, ghostly light, she couldn't be sure if the man was attractive or not, but he certainly smelled nice. "Hi," she said, smiling at him. "I apologise in advance for any screaming."

He shrugged, smiled back. "Me too."

She giggled, then turned and clasped the shoulders of the person in front of her. It was time. The member of staff pushed open a door and ushered them into a narrow corridor where the darkness was broken only by sporadic light from flashing strobe bulbs. Hands on shoulders, a line of tentative humans headed into the unknown.

***

A while later the group emerged into the gift shop, wild-eyed and letting out nervous giggles. The man who'd been at the front looked utterly embarrassed—at one point, when a large figure dressed as a villain from a slasher movie had jumped out on them wielding a chainsaw, he'd squealed and made a run for the nearest door, leaving his wife and son behind, much to the amusement of mostly everyone else.

Emmy herself was thoroughly delighted to be out of the Tombs. It had been a great deal scarier, more terrifying, than the first part of the attraction, and she could now see why people were given plenty of chances to back out. If she'd known precisely what she was letting herself in for, she sincerely doubted she'd have gone through with it. Dangling things, creepy noises, being jumped out on, the unknown... her nerves were shot.

"Christ, I need a drink," she muttered as she tried to get through the throng of people and to the exit.

"Yeah, me too," came a voice. She turned to see the man who had been behind her in the line. "Mind if I join you?"

"Of course not. I might even treat you for protecting me from the monsters." She smiled. In the proper light she could see that he was, in fact, *very* attractive. As well as being tall and well-built, he had a mop of curly black hair, big blue eyes and a smile gorgeous enough to make a woman's knees weak. Hers were already weak from the fear, so she couldn't tell if he was making it worse or not.

"Well then, I can't resist an offer like that. To the pub!"

They exited, laughing, into the daylight, and ducked into the first pub they saw.

"Right," Emmy said, making a beeline for a free table. "You sit here, I'll go get our drinks. What are you having?"

"Um, I dunno. What are you having?"

"Vodka and coke. Why, what difference does that make?"

"I didn't know if we were on beers, wines, spirits or whatever. If you're having vodka, I'll have the same. No ice, please. I'm chilled enough." He shuddered theatrically, and Emmy sniggered and sauntered to the bar. It was only when she'd placed the order and paid for the drinks that she realised she didn't even know the guy's name. Christ—her underground fright really had messed her head up!

She picked up the two vodkas and returned to the table, then handed her new friend his drink. "Here you go. By the way, what's your name?"

His eyes widened and his mouth dropped open. Then his sinful lips twisted into a grin. "Oh, shit, sorry! I can't believe we haven't done introductions. That bloody place has screwed with my mind." He held out his hand. "I'm Dylan."

"Emmy." They shook hands, and Emmy slid into the seat beside him. Dylan, huh? A cute name to go with a cute guy.

"Nice to meet you, Emmy. Thank you for the drink."

"You're welcome. Cheers." She clinked her glass against Dylan's, then downed the drink in one, closing her eyes as she felt the burn all the way down her throat and into her stomach. "Ahh. Delicious."

When she opened her eyes, Dylan was peering at her incredulously. "Wow, you needed that, didn't you? Was it really that bad?"

Nodding, she replied, "It was really that bad. I have an overactive imagination, which doesn't help. And don't pretend like you were some big, tough bloke, either. I heard your little squeaks every now and again. Not to mention the fingers digging into my shoulders!" She clipped his arm playfully.

"Shit, did you? Damn. Well, I suppose I'd better drown my sorrows in drink then, eh?" With that, he downed his vodka and Coke in one, then flashed her a grin. "A few more of those and The London Tombs will blur into oblivion. My round."

Before she could reply, he was out of his seat and striding over to the bar. She shrugged. Another wouldn't hurt. It wasn't like she had to drive anywhere. Though she should let Charis know what was going on, before she started to worry. She retrieved her phone from her pocket and sent her friend a quick text update, telling her she'd gone for a drink, then flipped the device onto silent and put it away.

When Dylan returned, they fell back into conversation and were soon laughing and joking once more. They discovered that, as well as both being petrified of what they'd just experienced, they had plenty more in common, too. Shared music tastes, TV programmes, a love of travel... they were certainly compatible. He seemed like a great guy.

If it weren't for the fact she lived nowhere near London and was just visiting, she'd definitely be up for dating Dylan and seeing where it went. Given that wasn't an option, though, she figured a one-night—or afternoon, anyway—stand would be a great alternative. She was fairly certain he liked her and would be up for it, so she decided to bite the bullet.

She finished her drink and put the empty glass down. "So, what do you want to do now? Want to get out of here?" Raising an eyebrow, she paired it with a grin that would leave him in no doubt as to what she was proposing.

"Uh, yes?" He drained his own glass, put it down, then spoke again. "Yes, absolutely. My place?"

With a nod, she took the hand he offered and allowed him to help her from her seat, then lead her from the pub. Once they were outside, she asked, "Do we need to stop somewhere and get protection, first?" It was an incredibly forward thing to say, but she didn't care. The last thing she wanted was to get back to his, start getting hot, heavy and naked, only to find that he didn't have condoms.

"No." He grinned. "It's all right, I've got some. And they're even in date."

She smirked back, then, as they continued walking, the smirk turned into a frown. Was he saying he didn't need condoms very often, which is why it was fortunate they were in date? In other words, he wasn't getting laid? Seriously, a hot guy like him, living in London, couldn't get a shag? Either that or he was in a committed relationship which meant he no longer needed the protection.

She stopped dead, right there on the pavement, causing tuts and sighs to emanate from the people behind them, forced to go around.

"Hey," Dylan said, his brow creasing, "are you all right?"

"I-I don't know," she said honestly, peering up at him.

"What's the matter? Tell me, please. If you've changed your mind, it's okay. I'm not going to force you into anything."

God, he just seemed so nice, so genuine. "I-it's just... I can't help wondering why a man like you has condoms in risk of going out of date."

He laughed, long and loud, then stopped abruptly. "Shit, you're serious, aren't you?"

Emmy nodded. "Yeah. Either you're not getting laid very often, which makes me question why, or you're in a long-term relationship, so you don't need them anymore."

Dylan's mouth dropped open. He looked as though he was going to speak, but nothing came out. He snapped his mouth shut, then opened it again. "You're very direct."

She shrugged. "I just like knowing what I'm getting myself into."

"Fair enough. That's commendable. Well, I'm definitely not in a long-term relationship. I'm not in *any* kind of romantic or sexual relationship—so you don't need to worry about that. I'm free and single. As for the not getting laid very often, well, you're absolutely right. I don't. With regards to the why, if I tell you, I'm not sure you'll believe me."

"Try me," she shot back, her voice dripping with sarcasm. Her enthusiasm for going home with Dylan was waning. Yes, he was hot and she fancied him like mad, but she had no wish whatsoever to get into bed with a nutter.

He sighed, then placed his hands on her shoulders and guided her over to one side of the pavement, out of the way of the milling crowds. "I'm shy, all right?" he said earnestly. "I find it incredibly difficult to chat up women, make the first move, whatever you want to call it. I've been very outlandish today, for me. I think it was the effects of the Tombs that made me blurt out about going for a drink with you. And when I've had some booze, well, things get easier. So here we are." Shrugging, he continued, "But if you've changed your mind, I'll understand."

Emmy frowned; examined his face, his body language. They indicated he was telling the truth and, after a beat, she realised she believed him. He was a nice guy, just shy under normal circumstances. And today had been far from normal.

"Okay," she said with a grin, "I believe you. Come on, let's go, before we ruin the mood entirely with our serious conversation."

Dylan took her hand and strode along the pavement in the direction of the Tube station, pulling her along behind him. She scurried to keep up, giggling and panting at the relentless pace. "Hey," she yelled, squeezing his fingers, "ease up! I'll end up going arse over tit at this rate."

After shooting her a glance over his shoulder, Dylan grinned and did as she asked. "Sorry. I'm just eager, that's all."

"That's a lovely compliment, thank you. But wouldn't you much rather get me there in one piece?"

"A good point, well made," he said, falling into step beside her. "It's not far, anyway."

Even at a normal pace, they reached his flat within fifteen minutes—a small but stylish place with floor-to-ceiling windows overlooking the Thames. She dreaded to think how much it cost. Probably more than a decent three-bedroomed property back home. "Nice place."

"Thanks. I think so."

As Emmy followed Dylan through the flat and into his bedroom, it was clear that not only was he stylish, he was tidy, too.

"Okay," he said, closing the door behind them. "Make yourself at home." He headed over to the window and reached for the cord to close the blinds.

"Wait," Emmy said, moving up behind him and grabbing his wrist. "Leave them open. Let's get rid of your shyness once and for all, shall we?"

A line appeared between his eyebrows. "W-what do you mean?"

"Go get a condom and I'll show you."

He stared at her for several seconds, seemingly trying to work out whether she was joking or not, then moved to his bedside cabinet and retrieved a foil packet from the top drawer.

"Good boy. Now give it to me." Emmy didn't know where her sudden bossy streak had come from—but she kinda liked it.

Taking the condom from him, she issued another order. "Get naked."

"W-what about you?"

"Once you're naked, I'm going to put this condom on you, then I'm going to take my clothes off."

"O-okay." Awkwardly, Dylan undressed, dropping each item into a pile at his feet as he went. His gaze flitted between her and the view behind her—presumably to make sure no one could see his state of undress. They were high up, but not so high that the outside world couldn't see what was going on, which of course was the point. Her gaze, on the other hand, remained firmly on him and the luscious body he revealed.

Once Dylan was naked, Emmy beckoned to him. He approached, and she immediately pulled his cupped hands away from his crotch and grasped his cock. It was almost at full hardness—despite his bashfulness, it seemed his hormones were doing their job—so she stroked it until it was raring to go, rubbered him up, and stripped off.

Then, with more than a flicker of disbelief at her own behaviour, she leaned against the window. She gasped as her skin hit the cold surface, then recovered herself and beckoned Dylan once more. "Come here, Mr. Posh-Flat-in-London, and fuck me."

Intense colour burned on his cheeks. He glanced out of the window, then back at her face. "But don't you want me to, er, get you turned on, first?"

"Oh, don't you worry about me," she purred, slipping a hand between her legs and discovering, as expected, that the booze and the situation had already got her plenty wet enough for penetration. And once they started fucking, she'd only get wetter.

Dylan looked unsure, so she grabbed his wrist and guided his hand to her pussy. He groaned as he encountered her heat and wetness, and she took the opportunity to slip her arms around his neck and pull him in for a kiss.

The thought that any one of hundreds—thousands

probably—of people in London could see her rear view, naked and rude, was incredibly arousing. She was aware she was being a little crazy and wouldn't be doing this if she was completely sober. But nor would she have sex with a stranger, either. Right in that second, though, there was nothing she wanted more. His intoxicating scent surrounded her, his warm body pressed against her, and his eager hardness was within inches of where she needed it most.

She reached down and grasped his cock, then manoeuvred it into position. Once it was at the right angle, she encouraged Dylan to push inside.

"Just a little," she said. "Then lift me up, hold on tight and fuck me hard."

She linked her hands together behind his neck as he obliged, cupping her bottom and lifting her. The movement forced his thick shaft deeper inside her, making them both groan. Once she'd wrapped her legs around him, securing her position, Dylan began to rock in and out of her cunt, steadily picking up his pace.

As Emmy slid up and down the glass, she couldn't help wondering what an interesting pattern would be left behind when they were done. Grinning at the thought, she slipped a hand down to play with her clit. It was already distended and incredibly sensitive, so it didn't take long to tease a climax from her body.

Every muscle tightened, and the tingle that had begun in her abdomen radiated out through every cell as she tumbled into blissful oblivion. Vaguely aware that her gripping cunt had pushed Dylan over the edge too, she began to laugh. And once she'd started, she couldn't stop. It was probably making Dylan awfully paranoid about his sexual prowess, but she just couldn't help it. It had been a supremely weird day, after all.

She'd gone from freaking out in a spooky tourist attraction deep underground to a delicious high-rise fuck with a stranger. She wasn't entirely sure how it had happened—but was incredibly glad it had. After disentangling from her sexy new friend, she pressed a kiss to his lips, grateful for his hands on her hips, steadying her. Her legs weren't ready to hold her up yet.

As she came down from the amazing orgasmic high, she wondered exactly how she was going to explain to Charis where she'd been for the past couple of hours. The truth was so bizarre her friend probably wouldn't believe it.

Oh, Brother!

I wasn't being entirely unselfish when I'd offered to give Marc a lift to his sister's housewarming party. His sister, Melanie, was my best friend and she'd recently bought a place with her bloke, Rob. She'd asked me if I could help out with the move, and, great friend that I am, I'd said yes. When I got to her old house to start packing boxes, I had the shock of my life.

Melanie's younger brother, Marc, walked into the front room carrying something. That in itself wasn't shocking, of course, but my jaw gaped unbecomingly nonetheless. The last time I'd seen him he'd been about eleven years old. He'd also had a crush on me, which at seventeen I'd found hilarious and gross all at once.

Now I found *I* was the one with the crush. At nineteen years of age, Marc had grown up into an incredibly good-looking guy. Gorgeous, actually. He was wearing low-cut jeans and a tight vest, which showed off his fit body to perfection. Melanie had gone off to make some drinks, so I found myself having a good old gawp at his muscular biceps and broad shoulders as he bent to put his burden down.

I snapped my gaze to his face as he straightened up and walked over to me, smiling. He bent to press a kiss on my cheek. "Hi, Lara. How are you? I haven't seen you in *years*. You look great!"

"I'm good, thanks," I said, a little flustered by his proximity, not to mention the compliment. "How about you? I can't believe how much you've changed. You were just a kid the last time I saw you."

"And now I'm towering over you. Did you stop growing, or something?" He quipped, his blue eyes sparkling with mischief.

I punched him on the arm. "Shut it, you. You're never too old for a slap."

"Ooh, yes please!"

The banter had continued all day, only wandering into flirt territory when Melanie was out of earshot. It hadn't gotten overly racy, but it was obvious there was something between us. I just didn't know how long we'd be able to ignore it.

***

Pulling up outside the flat Marc shared with some friends, I beeped the car's horn to announce my arrival. I flipped the sun visor down, quickly checking my reflection in its mirror. Catching movement out of the corner of my eye, I put the visor back up and looked over to see Marc walking towards my car. At that moment I knew I was doomed.

He wore smart jeans and shoes with a white shirt. His dark hair was in a fashionably messy style—the type that looked like no time at all had been spent doing it, but in reality it had probably taken him half an hour. He looked totally hot. Melanie would *not* be pleased if she knew what I was thinking at that moment.

I faced front as he got into the car, trying to avoid staring at something I shouldn't. When he was seated, his backside now safely out of view, I turned to say hi and got a smacker on the lips for my trouble. Marc jumped back. "S-sorry," he said, his face reddening, "I was aiming for your cheek, but you moved!"

Equally embarrassed, I waved a hand, trying not to make it a big deal. "Don't worry. These things happen. Belt up, then." With that I put the car in gear, released the handbrake and set off towards Melanie and Rob's new house.

Later that evening, I was trapped in a corner, being talked at by some boorish lawyer. Or he could have been an accountant—I'm not sure, because I wasn't listening. Sure, I was looking at him and nodding at what I thought were appropriate moments. But my mind was elsewhere. On Marc, to be exact.

I nonchalantly glanced around, my heart lurching when a pair of blue eyes caught my attention. Marc was looking in my direction. I smiled and rolled my eyes at the lawyer/accountant. Marc smirked in response.

My acquaintance hadn't even noticed I wasn't listening to him. Clearly he just liked the sound of his own voice. I looked back at Marc, who pointed to the patio doors leading out into the garden, then lifted his eyebrows in query. I nodded.

Making some excuse about needing the toilet, I walked away from the dullard, not bothering to wait for his reaction—if there even was one. I scooted towards the doors, then passed through them into the garden.

A couple of patio heaters were set up, meaning smokers could come outside to appease their cravings without freezing their arses off. It wasn't too cold, being mid-May, but the heaters lit the area too. Not that it helped me any. I looked around and couldn't see Marc anywhere. Then a noise had me squinting into the darkness beyond the decking area. I saw a movement and headed towards it.

Marc was skulking by the side of the house, where there was a space between the fence and the building. It was like an alleyway, but since it was fenced off at one end, that clearly wasn't its purpose. Knowing Melanie and Rob, it'd be full of garden junk in no time. For now, it was our hiding place. Marc grabbed my hand and pulled me down to the end of the alley where nobody could see us.

"What are you doing?" I hissed, blinking as my eyes adjusted to the darkness.

"Rescuing you from the boring guy. What was he going on about, anyway?"

"You didn't rescue me. I rescued myself! And I've no idea— I wasn't listening to a word he said."

"Well, I found you somewhere to hide, didn't I? It's like hide and seek!"

"Yes," I said dryly, "except nobody else is playing. It's just us."

We leaned against the house wall side by side. Tingles skated over my skin as he moved closer to me.

"Just us," he said, his lips right by my ear, his warm breath caressing my skin, "is that a problem?"

"N-no, I guess not."

He shuffled closer still, so our arms touched. His fingers groped for mine, and I let him take my hand. My heart thumped, and my mouth went dry. It was decision time. Could I really let this happen? He might be a grown man, but he was still my best friend's little brother.

"I always had a crush on you, you know," he murmured.

"I remember."

"But I was just a kid then. I'm not anymore, and it's obvious there's something between us."

I didn't respond. This guy had been eleven when I was seventeen. My best friend's little brother, for God's sake!

He moved to stand in front of me, then placed his hands on the wall either side of my head, forcing me to look at him. "Tell me I'm wrong."

"But Melanie..."

"Fuck Melanie. This is about us. Tell me you don't feel the same and I'll never mention it again."

Even in the gloom I could make out the longing and hope in his expression. And though my lips wouldn't form the words, my body was screaming them. My nipples were like tiny pebbles and the warmth between my legs was getting increasingly difficult to ignore. I felt the same, all right. I wanted him.

Fortunately, he didn't take my silence as a no. We maintained eye contact for several long seconds, the tension palpable. Something was obviously going to happen; it was just a matter of who would make the first move. By now, my pussy ached and my underwear was soaked.

Marc acted first. He bent his head and pressed a soft, closed-mouth kiss to my lips. Then he lingered, waiting for my reaction. Finally, my body overthrew my brain and I kissed him back, opening my lips to admit his tongue. I slipped my arms around his waist, grabbed his arse and pulled him to me. His hard cock pressed into my stomach, which sent a further jolt of lust to my hungry pussy.

Soon, I forgot about everything. I didn't know who I was, who he was; anything. All I knew was I was totally hot for this guy and I wanted him to fuck me—now. I put my hands on his waist and guided him around so his back was to the wall. I kicked his feet apart and stood between them. Following my lead, Marc slid down the wall a little so he was more my height.

Eagerly, I moved in for another kiss. At the same time I slid my hands under his shirt, then moaned into his mouth as my fingers contacted the delicious ridges of his abdomen. Moving further up, I swept my thumbs over his nipples which were erect and—judging from Marc's wriggling, gasping reaction—very sensitive. Pinching them lightly, I smiled as he groaned into my mouth. I ground my pussy against his crotch; getting more and more worked up as I thought about how it would feel inside me. The friction against my clit was amazing, but I wanted more. Needed it.

I gave Marc's nipples a vicious twist. He grunted, then grabbed me, spun us, and slammed my back against the wall. He kissed my neck as his fingers moved to undo my shirt buttons. I arched my back, desperate for him to touch my tits. He soon obliged, wrenching open my top, then pulling down the cups of my bra to expose my breasts to the night air.

My flesh puckered at the sudden change in temperature, but Marc was on the case. His hot, wet mouth enclosed one nipple as he brushed the flat of his hand across the other, teasing the already erect nub, making it grow harder still. I leaned my head against the wall as he pleasured me with hand and mouth.

The feel of his tongue and lips on my sensitive skin was sublime. I was so wet by this point I was in serious danger of making a damp patch on my jeans.

Marc trailed his mouth across my chest, then fastened onto the other nipple and slid his hand down to my fly. He popped open the button and pulled down the zip, making enough room to slide his hand inside. A millisecond later, I gasped as his cool hand touched my fevered skin.

Marc leaned his forehead against mine as his fingers played in my soaked slit. "God, you're wet," he said, tracing tiny circles around my distended nub, "I wanna fuck you so bad."

I said nothing, just parted my lips wantonly. He drove his tongue into my mouth, kissing me hungrily as he slipped two digits inside my clenching hole. Groaning, I writhed on his hand, wanting it deeper, faster. Marc obliged, roughly fingering my cunt as his tongue fucked my mouth. Frantic, I bucked my hips, and when he used the hand clamped to my pussy to shove me against the wall, the pressure triggered my climax.

Marc pulled away and delightedly watched my face as I came, pussy greedily grabbing at his fingers and soaking them with my juices. His other hand was busily releasing his cock from the confines of his jeans and boxers. By the time I'd calmed enough to form rational thought, he had his dick in his hand and was stroking it.

I grinned dopily at him, still high on endorphins. He smiled back, pulled his hand from my knickers and sucked my juices off his fingers. "Mmm," he said, making my pussy flutter with need. "That was so hot, Lara. I really need to fuck you now."

"You got a condom?" I replied, mentally crossing my fingers and toes that he'd give the right answer. When he nodded, I sighed with relief. "Then be my guest."

As he retrieved his wallet from his pocket, I hurriedly kicked off a shoe and pulled my jeans off one leg. It would have been much easier to do it doggy style, but I wanted to see his face. I'm sure I looked quite the trollop, standing in an alleyway with my shirt undone, boobs hanging out of my bra and my jeans bunched around one ankle, but I didn't care.

All I cared about was the cock currently having a condom rolled onto it, and the person it belonged to. As Marc made sure the rubber was firmly in place, I unbuttoned his shirt, craving the sensation of skin against skin. Then I used the sides of the shirt to pull him towards me.

Taken by surprise, he crashed into me. My arse scraped against the rough brick wall, but I didn't give a shit.

Marc captured my lips in another toe-curler of a kiss as he reached for my jean-less thigh. He manoeuvred my leg to rest over his arm, giving him easy access to my pussy. Using his other hand to position the tip of his cock at my entrance, Marc pulled away from our kiss, only to watch my face once more. Then he thrust into me.

My eyes widened and I clutched at his biceps as he stretched and filled me. My pussy clenched around his shaft, causing us both to moan at the sensation.

When he was in me to the hilt, Marc paused momentarily, catching his breath. Then he began to fuck me like he meant it. I was so wet squelching sounds filled the air. Coupled with the noise of skin against skin and the grunts and incoherent babble issuing from our lips, had anyone heard us there'd have been no mistaking what we were up to. Luckily, we weren't disturbed.

Marc's position meant, much to my delight, that every movement ground his pubic bone against my clit. Before long I was heading for my second orgasm, and I told him so.

"Well, I best catch up to you then, hadn't I?" Picking up his speed, Marc made short, hard thrusts into my willing body. My arse would have some serious scratches on it by the time we were done, but at that moment all I could think about was the tingling feeling filtering through me as I got closer to coming.

I clung onto Marc's arms for dear life as he screwed me, enjoying the feel of the firm muscles beneath my fingertips, as well as using them for leverage. But when I began to come, my fingernails dug into his skin, making him yell and hit his own peak.

Suddenly, I was a mass of physical sensation. My cunt went wild and I felt every twitch and leap of Marc's spurting cock deep inside me. My climax seemed to last forever, leaving me limp as I rode it out. Marc, apparently sensing this, released my leg and held me around the waist as I came back to myself. Resting his chin on my head, he waited until my breathing had steadied, then planted a kiss on my hair before pulling out of me, using a hand to ensure the condom stayed where it was supposed to be.

"You all right?" he asked, snapping off the rubber and stuffing it into the wrapper it had come out of.

I nodded weakly, still wrung out. "Just a little wobbly, that's all."

"In a good way, right?"

Smiling, I replied, "Right."

We dressed in silence. When we were decent, Marc crept to the garden end of the alley to check the coast was clear. He disappeared momentarily and I heard the open and close of a wheelie bin lid. Then he popped his head around the corner and beckoned to me.

By some miracle, we got back inside without anyone taking a second glance in our direction, or enquiring as to where we'd been. As we walked into the kitchen to grab drinks, Marc subtly brushed my back and whispered "Brick dust" into my ear, making us both grin like idiots.

Once I realised we'd got away with it, the memory of his mouth on my nipples and his cock plundering my pussy made me all hot and bothered again. It seemed one taste of my best friend's brother had left me hungry for more.

I was *so* fucked.

"Are you okay?" Marc asked, looking concerned. "You look a bit red."

I moved closer to him, ensuring nobody would hear what I said to him. "Wanna get outta here?"

Within minutes, we'd made our excuses and left, desperate to get our hands on each other again.

***

We'd promised to return the following morning to help with clean up. So, after a night of flatmate-pissing-off sex, I had to dash home early to get showered and changed before returning to Melanie and Rob's. Melanie didn't miss much—she'd definitely notice if I turned up in yesterday's clothes. And, given I'd left with her brother, it wouldn't take a genius to figure out what had happened.

Luckily, the morning passed without much incident. There was a hairy moment when Marc and I carried some bags to the wheelie bin and saw the condom wrapper staring up at us. We smirked at one another, then our gazes flicked to the alleyway. Unable to control ourselves, we started to giggle.

Melanie, ever the slave driver, came to see what was taking us so long and caught us red-faced and laughing in her garden. She sighed and told us to stop messing around or there'd be no bacon sandwiches—our promised reward for helping clean up. Suitably chastised, we pulled it together, the occasional smirk and sidelong glances getting us through the rest of Operation Cleanup.

It was the longest morning of my life. I was still buzzing with that I-had-amazing-sex feeling and I just wanted to finish so I could drag Marc back into bed. Needless to say, there was no more messing about. We ate our bacon sarnies and were out of there like lightning.

***

We haven't got around to telling Melanie yet. We're at her house a lot, helping with gardening, decorating and the like. She thinks I pick Marc up because his place is en-route to hers. If she actually knew that most weekends we just tumble out of bed and into the car, she probably wouldn't be so welcoming. Still, we'll cross that bridge when we come to it.

Desperate Measures

Recession. Credit crunch. Inflation. Poppy was fed up of
hearing the words. She didn't need to keep seeing the news reports
to know the depressing truth. She—and many other people besides—
was broke. Before the financial crisis hit, Poppy had been doing just
fine. Really well, actually. She'd had a great job as a project
manager at a firm that worked with chain supermarkets. Granted, it
had meant there were occasional late-night phone calls to deal with,
but the money had been good enough that the interruptions were
worth it. The nice house, car and luxurious holidays had also kept
her smiling through the busy periods when she was ready to rip some
incompetent contractor's head off.

Unfortunately, money problems had affected everyone and
made them tighten their belts, including the supermarkets. As a
result, Poppy was out of a job. Various schemes she'd paid into over
the years ensured she still had a roof over her head, thankfully; but
the luxuries she'd previously enjoyed were no longer an option.

Naturally, she'd thrown herself into job hunting as soon as
she'd found out she was being made redundant. But people with her
skill set and experience were expensive, and companies were getting
rid of expensive and not-absolutely-necessary people, not taking
them on.

The monthly repayments on her mortgage were high, and
while she was on jobseeker's allowance they were being paid for
her. Poppy was no snob, but she couldn't afford to take just *any* job
because as soon as she became employed again, the insurance
company would stop paying her mortgage. Therefore, if her new job

paid a lot less than her previous one, she'd end up even worse off than she was now. She was in a serious dilemma. If only she could find a way to earn some extra cash while she was looking for a job, then she wouldn't have to dip into her hard-earned savings.

One evening, as she surfed job websites looking for possible roles, Poppy sat back in her chair and sighed with resignation. Her search was proving fruitless, and it was really beginning to get her down. But then, as her gaze landed on the gadget hooked onto the top of her computer monitor, her eyes narrowed and inspiration hit. She jerked forward again and began frantically googling. A little while later, Poppy's genius plan was in action.

She'd need a few props, of course, but that wasn't an issue. Before she'd been made redundant, sex toys, kinky costumes and the like had been some of the 'luxuries' Poppy had splashed her cash on. Now she was going to put them to good use to get her out of a sticky situation. It wasn't exactly what she'd envisioned doing, but as the saying went, desperate times call for desperate measures. Plus, she'd always been a bit of an exhibitionist—she might even enjoy it.

In her bedroom, Poppy knelt and reached under the bed to pull out two big boxes, one after the other. She'd bought so much stuff over the years—she was a sucker for sales and '3 for 2' offers—that she couldn't remember exactly what she owned. Her trusty rabbit, of course, was in the bedside cabinet for easy access when it was needed. And in her current single and jobless status, it was needed pretty damn frequently.

She started with the costume box. Her highest priority— besides pocketing some cash, obviously—was hiding her identity.

The last thing she needed was this coming to bite her on the arse in the future. She was suddenly glad she'd never gotten a tattoo; an identifying mark if ever there was one. After a moment, she pulled something out of the box with a grin. It was perfect. Everything else was secondary. The mask meant she was ready to become a webcam girl. In secret, of course.

The mask was the type one would wear to a masquerade ball. It was a beautiful deep red colour, overlaid with grey lace and black sequins. Not that the way it looked mattered. The important thing was that it would conceal Poppy's identity. She stood and moved over to her dressing table with its large mirrors. After slipping the mask on, she nodded in satisfaction. It would be a miracle if anyone recognised her while wearing it. Excellent.

By the time Poppy had finished rooting through all her various toys and props and gone back to her computer, the new account on the webcam chat site she'd signed up for had been approved. All she had to do now was set up an anonymous profile, add a photo, post an ad and wait for the offers to come in.

It didn't take long. The photo she'd posted wasn't brilliant quality, as she'd taken it with the webcam and uploaded it directly, but it sure was sexy. After closing the curtains and checking there was nothing to identify her within sight, she'd posed in the mask, some sexy black lingerie and a matching feather boa. It had obviously done the trick. The first message simply said *u r very sexy,* so she deleted it immediately. She wouldn't tolerate time wasters. When the site refreshed, she already had another note in her inbox. It was much more promising, too.

Hi Jane0874, it said, *love that profile pic. You are gorgeous. Would love to have some fun with you. So what do you do, and how much?*

That gave Poppy pause. What *did* she do? She was limited as to what she could do to herself in front of a camera—so what to say? And how much to charge?

After a few minutes' consideration, she typed out a reply. *Hi Jase69*—she had to snigger at the name—*why not make me an offer?*

She hit 'send' and sat back to wait. A reply came back almost instantly.

How about a striptease? £10?

Poppy grinned. This guy was easily pleased. He was also going to get the performance of a lifetime. She'd once attended a workshop at a nearby women's sex emporium on how to drive a man wild with a striptease. After the initial embarrassment of doing it in front of complete strangers, and a couple of glasses of wine, Poppy had actually enjoyed herself. She'd dashed home after the class and demonstrated her new-found skills to her boyfriend at the time. He'd been *very* impressed; even slipping a £20 note into the front of her G-string, then waiting until she was completely naked and fucking her brains out right there on the living room floor. She'd had carpet burns for days afterwards.

Having answered Jase69 in the affirmative, Poppy looked around the room. It was used as an office, so was functional and tidy rather than seductive. She pursed her lips thoughtfully and picked up the webcam to see how long the lead was that attached it to the computer. Not very long at all. It certainly wasn't long enough to reach through to her bedroom. Shrugging, Poppy decided it would have to do for now. She could always get an extension lead if her money-making scheme took off.

As she put the webcam back in its original position, her email pinged. She quickly opened the new message, raising her eyebrows as she took in the content. This was going to be easier than she thought. She'd received a donation from Jase69, and she hadn't even done anything yet. She fired off a quick confirmation message, then dashed into her bedroom to get ready. The black lingerie and feather boa she'd worn to take her profile photo were fine, but she needed more layers to strip out of, or it really wouldn't be much of a tease.

Poppy quickly selected her outfit and pulled it on. She scrutinised herself in the mirror, figuring she would do. It wasn't particularly original, but the nurse's uniform was an old faithful that most guys loved. In future she'd list the dress-up options and give 'customers' the choice, but for now this would have to do. Given the way the neckline of the skimpy dress pushed her tits up and out, Poppy was pretty sure she'd have no complaints. She couldn't get the cap on over her mask, so she just swapped the feather boa for the fake stethoscope, added a pair of sexy stilettos and strutted back into the office.

Poppy flicked on the webcam, then messaged Jase69 to let him know she was ready. He must have been waiting, as mere seconds later a little icon appeared in the messaging window. She squinted at it, then frowned. After a beat, the penny dropped. The picture was of two tiny hands giving the thumbs up gesture. Smiling, she nodded at the camera, then clicked play on the track she'd chosen to dance to. She stepped back into a position where her entire body would be visible in the camera. As soon as the song started properly, she counted in the beats, then began her routine.

The sensual yet upbeat track she'd chosen gave her ample opportunity to shake her arse, Shakira-style, while smoothing her hands seductively up and down her body. After a while, she realised if she didn't get a move on, she'd still be fully clothed when the song ended. So, slowly, erotically, she unzipped the naughty nurse dress to reveal more and more cleavage, then her bra. She stopped halfway, flashing a coy smile at the webcam and shimmying around some more before dragging the zip all the way down to reveal her gently curved stomach and tiny G-string.

Pulling the sides of the dress apart, Poppy swayed to the beat. Had there been a man in front of her at this point, she'd have straddled him. Thinking on her feet, she grabbed her computer chair and twirled it to face her. Then she proceeded to pretend the chair was her customer, leaning forward and pushing her tits together.

As she flicked her gaze up to the computer screen, Poppy saw a series of new messages had appeared. Line after line held smiley faces, smileys with their tongues hanging out, more thumbs up, and finally some text: *Typing with one hand now.*

Poppy arched an eyebrow and carried on with what she was doing—apparently she was doing a good job. She gyrated and wiggled on the chair, then stood abruptly and cast off the dress. Turning her back to the camera, she thrust out her arse and stroked it as she moved, tantalising her viewer with what he could see but couldn't touch. She turned back, played with the stethoscope, pushing her breasts together with her elbows at the same time. Pouting at her unseen audience, Poppy then tossed the prop to the floor and reached around to undo her bra.

She removed the garment as slowly as possible, then rolled her shoulders, making her tits jiggle as they were revealed. As the bra hit the carpet, Poppy covered her breasts with her hands—well, as much as she could with 38Es and relatively small hands—then spread her fingers teasingly, allowing the milky flesh to spill and peek out from between them. As she squeezed and pinched, Poppy wasn't entirely surprised when her nipples poked against her palms. She was supposed to be turning someone else on—yet it was having quite the favourable effect on her, too.

Sliding her hands down her stomach and out to her hips, Poppy then hooked her thumbs into the sides of her G-string. She pulled them out, then released them to snap against her skin. Turning her back to the webcam once more, she began to lower the scanty underwear as slowly as she could, all the while swaying and bopping her hips to the music. She kept hold of the G-string as she let it all the way down, so by the time it was around her ankles, she was bent right over and giving Jase69 a lewd view of her arse cheeks and the swollen pussy lips peeking out from between them. As the air played across her vulva, Poppy realised just how aroused she was and wondered if her viewer could see the juices that were seeping from her core.

She straightened, then lifted each leg in turn to step free of the underwear, then faced the camera yet again. Although she could no longer afford to keep her regular waxing appointments, Poppy had done the next best thing. The hair on her pubis was shaven into a neat landing strip which she stroked, before allowing her hand to dip right between her slightly parted legs and touch her slick pussy. Then, bringing her hand up to her face, she put her index and middle fingers into her mouth and sucked off all her cream. When she pulled her fingers back out of her mouth, she grinned smugly at the webcam as though to say *bet you wish you could do that, don't you?*

Knowing the song was almost at an end, Poppy repeated some of her breast-cradling and butt-wriggling moves before bending down to pick up the discarded G-string. Then, as the last bars of the music played, she shimmied towards the computer and gave a cheeky wave before draping the underwear over the camera lens. Only when the speakers had fallen silent did Poppy switch off the webcam and remove the obstruction.

With a huff, Poppy yanked off the mask and dropped it onto the desk. Her message window was overflowing. She reached for the mouse, and had to scroll back up in order to read the first message after the 'typing with one hand' one. It read: *Fucking hell, you're good at this.*

Poppy smiled and continued reading. The lines of text, predictably, grew more and more explicit, just as her striptease had: *You have the most stunning body.*

Oh my god, I'd love to be touching that perfect arse right now.

Your tits are delicious. I'd love to stick my cock between them so you could give me a tit wank.

Would love to bite and suck your nipples.

Wow....

Your pussy looks wet. I'd love to stick my tongue into your tight snatch and lick you until you came all over my face.

Love the landing strip. I'd like to stroke my cock over it before plunging into your wet cunt.

Fuuuuuuuuck!

She'd been turned on already, but Poppy got more and more aroused as she read what Jase69 had been typing as he no doubt stroked his cock to orgasm. The last one in particular made a gush of juice seep from her pussy and soak her inner thighs. He'd clearly been right on the edge of coming. She smiled.

Just as she was about to turn away from the computer and go and get out her trusty rabbit, another message arrived: *Jane, that was absolutely incredible. I can't remember the last time I came so hard or so much.*

The ache in Poppy's pussy indicated it wouldn't be long before she was doing the exact same thing. But first, Jase69 had a request. *Same time tomorrow?*

The clock in the corner of the computer screen revealed the whole exchange had taken less than ten minutes. £10 for less than ten minutes? She could live with that. She shot a quick agreement to Jase69, then hurried into her bedroom, kicked off her shoes, retrieved her vibrator, and collapsed onto the bed.

As the bright pink shaft slipped easily into her saturated core and the bunny ears pressed against her swollen clit, Poppy had a thought.

If she could earn that kind of money doing a simple

striptease, what kind of money could she bring in for using her vibrator and other toys?

As her body ramped up to a speedy and intense orgasm, Poppy decided she wasn't so eager to get back to work after all.

Miss Pemberton's Drawers

Owen whistled as he worked. He wasn't sounding a particular tune—he was just making a noise, really, to mask the silence. This was the first time the children had been off since he'd started work in the school, so he was used to constant din in the building. Even during lessons he'd always been able to hear the murmur of voices from classrooms, toilets flushing and someone's footsteps as they click-clacked down a lonely corridor. But now, there was nothing, except for the occasional groans and creaks one always hears in a building.

It was eerie. As an ex-army private, he'd always had a pretty noisy workplace—some times more than others. But, he reminded himself, that was why he was here. He'd been injured in active service, and although it wasn't bad enough—thank God—to put him in a wheelchair or even on crutches, he couldn't be on the front line any longer. He'd been offered an office job in the army, but there was no way he wanted to do that. He'd never be able to cope with sitting behind a desk, knowing his friends and colleagues were out there on manoeuvres, it just wasn't *him*. So he'd left the army and got a simple job that wouldn't be too taxing and would earn him a few quid while he figured out what to do next. Therefore, he was currently in the position of caretaker in a secondary school and was pottering around during the school holidays, finding things that needed to be fixed, replaced or painted.

Thankfully, there was plenty to be getting on with, or he'd have been bored out of his mind, particularly with there being nobody around to talk to. At least in term time he exchanged the odd word with the teachers and other staff, and put up with good-natured jibing from the cockier kids. Though that had soon stopped when they found out he was an ex-soldier. He didn't know if it was fear or respect that kept them quiet, but either way he was pleased—he never knew how to respond, anyway. If he told them off or answered back they might go running to the headteacher, and although he knew the school wouldn't take the kids seriously, he'd rather not draw any attention to himself. He just wanted to get on with his job with the minimum of fuss while he figured out his future plans. So that's what he did. Kept his head down, remained polite with the teachers and staff, ignored the kids as much as possible.

Despite being a little rattled by the lack of sound, Owen was enjoying the solitude. He didn't have to worry about being polite or respectful to anyone, and he could get on with his tasks without having to check if certain areas of the building were being used first. As amusing as he would find it, he knew there'd be hell to pay if a load of kids went home with wet paint on their clothes because they'd leaned on the wrong door frame.

Having finished his current task, he checked his list. He'd grouped the tasks by room or area of the school, and saw that his next port of call was the art department. More specifically, Miss Pemberton's classroom. The woman seemed to be a walking catastrophe—she was always reporting broken chairs, wobbly tables, drawers that wouldn't shut... the list was endless. As a result, Owen spent quite a lot of time in her classroom. He didn't mind, though. Not only did she keep him busy, but she was mighty fine to look at, too.

She was younger than the other teachers—and himself—and it showed. Her laidback attitude was a world away from the rest of the stuffy faculty. She looked not unlike an art student, with her often paint-stained jeans and figure-hugging scruffy T-shirts. She was popular amongst the students, particularly the boys, and Owen could see why—he'd copped an eyeful of her bountiful breasts in those clingy tops on more than one occasion himself.

He took his toolbox over to his supply cupboard, then put it down and pulled open the cupboard door. He grabbed a clean paintbrush—which he stuffed in the back pocket of his overalls—and a tin of paint. After closing the door, he picked up his toolbox in his free hand and headed towards the art department. Time to see what damage Miss Pemberton had done this time.

Once outside the classroom door, Owen turned and pushed against it with his backside, rather than putting something down. Luckily it was unlocked, and the door opened, allowing him entrance. Whistling again, he moved quickly into the room, ready to start work.

He came to an abrupt stop on discovering he wasn't alone. Miss Pemberton was sitting at her desk, looking at him with an expression of surprise. Judging by the piles of paper in front of her, he'd interrupted her work.

"Oh, sorry," he said, backing towards the door, "I didn't realise you were here. I was going to take care of the stuff that needs doing in here, but I'll come back another day."

She stood then, and unless Owen was quite mistaken, her tits swung free, bra-less, beneath her low-cut vest top. "No," she said, forcing Owen's attention from her chest to her face, "it's okay. I'm only working here because I'm having a new kitchen fitted at home, and all the banging and drilling is driving me crazy. You're not going to be making much noise, are you?"

Owen dug his list out of his pocket and consulted it. "No, not really. I have to take a look at a couple of chairs, but I can always take them somewhere else, or come back later to do those. Other than that, I'll mainly be painting the skirting boards, the doors and frames, and the window frames. So other than when I'm taping up the stuff I don't want to paint on, I'll be pretty quiet."

She nodded. "Do you need some help moving the furniture?"

Owen looked around, figuring out where it would be best to start work. He decided to start with the door, so then it could be drying while he painted everything else and he wouldn't have to touch it for a while. "I'm okay for now, I think. But I'll let you know. Thanks."

She smiled, and, not for the first time, Owen thought about how much she resembled a pixie. With her cropped brunette hair, big green eyes, cheeky smile and petite figure, he could easily imagine her getting up to mischief in the woods. Preferably with him, he thought, turning rapidly away from her before his stiffening cock made itself apparent.

Desperate to distract himself from his dirty thoughts, and the fact that the seriously sexy art teacher was mere feet away from him, he got down to work as quickly as possible, flipping open his toolbox and grabbing the masking tape before moving towards the door.

He'd taped the edges of the panes of glass in the door and was just about to remove the handle when he heard a voice close behind him.

"I was wondering," Miss Pemberton said, looking into his eyes as he spun around to face her, "if you'd mind taking at a look at my drawers."

The slight smirk curling the corners of her lips told Owen she was well aware of the double entendre in her words. But what did she actually mean? Was she coming on to him, or did she genuinely want him to look at the huge sets of drawers which held the pupils' artwork? If he headed for the wooden drawers, she might think he wasn't interested, but equally, if he grabbed her and had got it wrong, he could end up with a slap and the loss of his job. Not to mention potential police involvement.

Frozen in place by his indecision, he stared at her. A glimpse at her chest told him she was either cold, or aroused. And given it was a glorious August day, he suspected the latter and concluded that she was indeed coming on to him.

He took a step towards her to see what she would do. She didn't move, so he grinned and said, "Could you point me in the direction of the drawers you would like me to look at?"

"Certainly," she said, beaming back up at him. "I'd be happy to… Owen."

Her utterance of his name made him realise he only knew her as Miss Pemberton. He was about to ask her what her first name was, but the action of her moving in front of him and grabbing his wrist made the thought fly from his head, to be replaced with much naughtier ones. Particularly when she used her other hand to undo her jeans, before pulling him towards her and shoving his hand between the parted flaps of denim.

"There," she cooed, fixing him with a look that could only be described as devilish, "those are the drawers that need looking at. Do you think you can help?"

Delving deeper, he pushed his fingers inside her underwear—which were less drawers and more dental floss—and sought her pussy. Following her flirtatious behaviour, he wasn't surprised to find her wet. A blissful moan came from her lips as he touched her hot, engorged flesh.

Remembering that she'd asked him a question, he murmured, "Yes, I think I can help. What seems to be the problem?" He stroked her swollen lips, then dipped between them to smear some of her copious juices across her clit.

"Well," she practically gasped, blinking rapidly and gripping his biceps to steady herself, "I seem to have trouble getting them to open."

"That so?" Owen was suddenly very glad he always carried a condom in his wallet. "Well, I'll do my best to solve your problem. If you could just..." He paused as he tried to think of further drawer-related entendres. Failing, he pulled his hand from her crotch, picked her up, walked across the room and deposited her on the biggest table. "Bollocks to all that, love. I'm fed up of talking now. Get your drawers off!"

She giggled. "I will if you will."

Owen responded by undoing the front of his overalls,

dropping them to the floor and stepping out of them. Quickly, he yanked down his tracksuit bottoms and boxer shorts, letting his cock spring free. He then snatched up the overalls and rummaged around in the pockets for his wallet, and the all-important protection. By the time he'd found the condom, Miss Pemberton had stripped off and was sitting up on the table, waiting for him.

"Eager, aren't we?" he joked, carefully tearing open the condom wrapper.

"Hell, yes," she responded, moving her hand to touch herself, "I've waited long enough. And, by the looks of it, it was worth the wait." She nodded towards his engorged cock.

"What do you mean, waited long enough?" He rolled the rubber down his erection, checking it was in place properly before approaching the table, then grabbing her ankles and pulling her so her bottom was at the edge.

"You're joking, aren't you?" She gasped as Owen pushed her hand out of the way and stroked the tip of his prick up and down her slick labia. "Haven't you ever wondered why there are always so many jobs for you to do in here?"

"Actually," he replied, then bit his lip with the effort of not thrusting into her, "I thought you were just a walking catastrophe. You know, a bit of a clumsy bitch. Hot, but clumsy."

She giggled, hooking her feet around his arse and pulling him closer, so the length of his shaft pressed tightly against the seam of her cunt. "Nope. I've had my eye on you ever since you started here. I enjoy watching you and your bulging muscles as you work. You've entertained me massively over the past couple of months."

Owen snorted, realising he'd been tricked. "So, let me guess, you don't have workmen in at home, either? You just came in, knowing I'd be working through the school holidays?"

"Oh no," she shook her head, "I really do have workmen in, but it just so happens my favourite workman is *here*, so I thought I'd drop by and see him."

"Well," he said, grasping his shaft and aiming it at her entrance, "I'm very glad you did. Now, I'm going to open your drawers, all right?" He grinned, and she nodded enthusiastically.

"It's more than all right. Please, Owen, fuck me." She used her legs to pull him into her as she spoke, and the room quickly filled with moans and groans as Owen's cock sunk balls-deep into her pussy.

He paused for a few seconds, enjoying the sensation of tight, hot wetness around his shaft. Her hips lifted, which he took as a hint to get on with it. Shifting into a better position, he then began to rock, giving sharp, short thrusts, and rolling his hips so her clit was stimulated on each stroke.

She clearly appreciated the effort, as before long she was gasping and clinging onto his biceps for dear life, her head thrown back and eyes squeezed tightly shut. "Uh... uh... Owen, I'm gonna, uh, come soon."

Her internal muscles squeezed him, proving her words to be true. He picked up his pace, knowing he wouldn't be far behind her. He was careful not to fuck her too hard, conscious of the hard surface beneath her body, but at the same time eager to please.

And please he did, if her physical reactions were anything to go by. Small contractions gripped and released his cock, and she stiffened beneath him, letting out a wail and digging her nails tightly into his arms. The pressure around his shaft increased, and he forced himself more deeply into her even as her pussy tried to push him out. The incredible sensation tipped him over the edge, and he came, yelling unintelligible sounds as his cock twitched and spurted its release inside the condom.

Careful not to crush her with his weight, Owen leaned down and captured Miss Pemberton's swollen mouth in a kiss. Her eyes fluttered open and crinkled at the corners as she eagerly reciprocated. It was a chaste kiss—both of them too breathless for anything more—and soon Owen pulled away and rolled onto the table next to her. She twisted her head to look at him, and they grinned at each other, basking in the afterglow of their respective orgasms.

After a few minutes, when he'd regained his presence of mind and the ability to speak, Owen said, "So, er, Miss Pemberton, was this a one-off thing, or what?"

"Bloody hell, don't call me Miss Pemberton. You sound like one of my pupils! It's Sally. And actually," she smirked, "if you're willing, I was wondering if you'd like to check my drawers on a more regular basis."

Owen laughed. "Is the sky blue? Though maybe we shouldn't make fucking on school property a regular occurrence, eh? I need this job."

"Agreed. Next time, you'll have to make a home visit."

"I charge a call out fee, you know."

"Would a blow job cover it?"

"Abso-fucking-lutely. You can pay in advance, if you like." He thrust his hips towards her, drawing her attention to his cock, which was stiffening again.

"Do you know," she slid off the table and shoved him onto his back before lowering her head towards his crotch, "I think I'll do that."

Owen crossed his arms behind his head, his grin spreading from ear to ear as Sally swallowed his cock. Maybe working during the school holidays wasn't so bad, after all.

***

A note from the author: Thank you so much for reading *Multi-Orgasmic Vol 2*. If you enjoyed it, please do tell your friends, family, colleagues, book clubs, and so on. Also, posting a short review on the retailer site you bought the book from would be incredibly helpful and very much appreciated. There are lots of books out there, which makes word of mouth an author's best friend, and also allows us to keep doing what we love doing—writing.

About the Author

Lucy Felthouse is the award-winning author of erotic romance novels *Stately Pleasures* (named in the top 5 of Cliterati.co.uk's 100 Modern Erotic Classics That You've Never Heard Of, and an Amazon bestseller), *Eyes Wide Open* (winner of the Love Romances Café's Best Ménage Book 2015 award, and an Amazon bestseller), *The Persecution of the Wolves, Hiding in Plain Sight* and *The Heiress's Harem* series. Including novels, short stories and novellas, she has over 170 publications to her name. Find out more about her writing at **http://lucyfelthouse.co.uk**, or on **Twitter (@cw1985)** or **Facebook (http://www.facebook.com/lucyfelthousewriter)**. Join her **Facebook group (https://www.facebook.com/groups/lucyfelthousereadergroup)** for exclusive cover reveals, sneak peeks and more! Sign up for automatic updates on **Amazon (http://author.to/lucyfelthouse)** or **BookBub (https://www.bookbub.com/authors/lucy-felthouse)**. Subscribe to her newsletter here: **http://www.subscribepage.com/lfnewsletter**

If You Enjoyed Multi-Orgasmic Vol 2

If you enjoyed this erotica collection, you may enjoy the books I've listed below. My full backlist is on **my website (http://lucyfelthouse.co.uk)**.

Multi-Orgasmic

From the pen of award-winning erotica author Lucy Felthouse comes a collection of short stories and flash fiction sure to hit the spot.

There's something for everyone nestling between the pages of this sexy anthology. From spanking to voyeurism, bondage to pegging, solo loving to ménage, with a sprinkling of femdom, maledom and magic, fans of M/F erotic stories will soon discover why this book is described as multi-orgasmic.

Enjoy twenty-one titillating tales, over 52,000 words of naughtiness packed into one steamy read.

Please note: Many of the stories in this book have been previously published in anthologies and online, but three of the tales are brand new and never seen before!

More information and buy links: **https://lucyfelthouse.co.uk/published-works/multi-orgasmic/**

Classic Felthouse

Fancy a blast from the past? Then dip in to five short stories from the Lucy Felthouse archive. A handful of her earliest published tales have been polished up and presented to you in one seriously hot collection. Enjoy a sexy soldier, a buxom babe, erotic daydreams, filthy phone sex and a language barrier, and see where it all began for this prolific author of erotica and erotic romance.

More information and buy links: **https://lucyfelthouse.co.uk/published-works/classic-felthouse-stories-from-the-archive/**

Caught in the Act

Police Constable David Beckett is just a normal guy, living a quiet life. His only excitement comes from his job—and even that's not exactly been a barrel of laughs just lately. That is until his colleagues burst into the office one morning, full of tales from the night shift. Tales that cause Dave's curiosity to get the better of him. Some idle surfing on the Internet opens up a whole world that Dave never knew existed—and he's fascinated. After watching an amateur video, things escalate quickly and Dave finds himself drawn into a kinky lifestyle that could cost him his reputation—and his job.

More information and buy links: **https://lucyfelthouse.co.uk/published-works/caught-in-the-act/**